# Young Adults Visit Other Dimensions

## The Secret World of the Plant People, Volume 4

Peter Brighton

Published by Peter Brighton, 2022.

YOUNG ADULTS VISIT OTHER DIMENSIONS

**First edition. November 15, 2022.**

Copyright © 2022 Peter Brighton.

ISBN: 979-8215655252

Written by Peter Brighton.

# Also by Peter Brighton

**FILM AND TV SCRIPTS SHORT STORIES**
Peter Brighton's Film Scripts Stories

**The Secret World of the Plant People**
The Secret World of the Plant People
The Secret World of Dream Children
The Secret World of Dream Animals and Plants
Young Adults Visit Other Dimensions

**Standalone**
Three Strangers Rob a Gangster
Seven Strangers Shadowed by Homeland Security

Watch for more at https://petersbooklets.com/.

# Table of Contents

Thank you, Draft2Digital support team, for helping me publish six books for free.

Also, thank you Dave Chesson of Kindlepreneur, and Ricardo Fayet of Reedsy for sending me many emails explaining how to promote my books.

Thank you Saqib Mushtaq. Known as Wshopia1319 on Fiverr for designing this book cover and three others of my books that I so enjoyed seeing. .

# INTRODUCTION

Like my previous Plant World Books. The characters in this story are mostly dream children entering Plant World where they use their individual skills and talents to help all living things when exploring the land that is similar to their human world. But there is no crime, anger, or even money. Plus, they can communicate with all living things. There are also stories about some dream children, and animal entering other dimensions that are unlike the human world. As they are spiritual energies that can mentally create anything they want or meet others from other worlds and centuries. Nor do they do not need to eat or drink.

(I suggest you keep a notepad and pen beside your bed when you go to sleep. Then when you wake up, try and record what your dreams were about. Some of your dreams may inspire you to write stories).

I have also added a story about a human who discovered the world of Lumarians who created an underground world thousands of centuries ago. But the world is still here as explained at the end of the story. I recommend you access the website of the science fiction writer Robert Graham who has written many stories about Lumerians, as well as, stories about Seth, the multi-dimensional educator.

# VISITOR ONE-REX THE PILOT AND PLANE DESIGNER.

A young teenage boy arrived in Plant World. His father, in the human world, had dreamt about him taking over his garage repair business. Because he had been helping him to repair cars and motorbikes.

He found himself in a workshop full of engines that he began to study. He then started to repair any that weren't working. For centuries Plant people had ridden horses, and built wagons to move around the country. But more and more children began arriving that wanted to explore continents a lot quicker. So, they started building road vehicles. But they always drove carefully to make sure they never hit any animal or crushed any plants.

He left the workshop and began cycling on a yellow cycle he had found. He started to ride along a narrow lane alongside a steep hillside. When suddenly, he heard a voice in his mind shout.

"Stop immediately. Squeeze the brakes" which he did.

To his amazement a large heavy boulder rolled in front of him. Then down into the valley below. Had he carried on cycling he would have been crushed. He wondered who had shouted at him to stop. But didn't spot anyone. So, he carried on cycling until he came across a hill with lots of large birds flying from tree to tree. He thought that he would also like to fly. But wondered how he could do so. He returned to the workshop where he met Uncle Twotrees and asked him how he could fly.

Uncle Twotrees suggested he went to sleep and dreamt he could fly. But to ask his consciousness to show him how he could fly when he woke up. He also told him that he was going to call him Rex the pilot. Rex in the human world meant 'King' and he foresaw that he was going to be considered king of plant world fliers.

Rex did what he was told and fell asleep. He didn't realize that he moved in his dream world to a dimension called Framework five. It is a world where people from other dimensions visit to meet people with skills and talents that they want to use. For example. Many artists go there to meet famous artists from previous centuries, such as, Michelangelo, and Picasso.

Rex found himself sitting with the brothers Orville and Wilbur Wright. They invented the first airplane that they explained how they did so, to Rex. Then two others joined them. One was Hans von Chain a former German who invented the Heinkel airplane, and Frank Whittle who designed the first turbojet. They all handed him papers explaining what they did. To his utter amazement he found them beside his bed when he woke up. He then took them to the workshop and began building the turbo jets. He met with Widget, the famous handyman in Plant world, who arranged for many skilled friends to start building an airplane designed by Rex.

When it was built. Rex dreamt how to fly it. He found himself as a co-pilot in dreamworld being taught how to take off, fly, then land on different looking pieces of land. When he woke up, he wandered over to the newly built plane and climbed in the pilot's seat. Hundreds of plant people were watching him take off. He pressed a number of buttons and heard the engines on each wing begin revving. He then slowly moved the airplane towards a runway that had been built. Then, revved up the engine and began hurtling along the runway. Then up into the sky.

He was utterly amazed at the height he was travelling and the brilliant view of the land and ocean below. He quickly moved from one continent to another before returning to the runway. It was not easy landing and stopping but he did so. Everyone, cheered him as he climbed from the airplane.

From then on. Not only did he go flying each day but he encouraged others to join him, as passengers. Some of whom joined him in the cockpit and learned to fly. When he returned to the airfield, he began designing many other airplanes, that they built in his workshop which is close to the Old Oak Garden center. Over time, he began to fly all over the world with passengers who left the airplane to teach locals how to build airfields.

Rex visited Africa which he really liked. So, he stayed there for many years. He also designed an airplane that could carry many different animals that needed help. As I've mentioned Plant People communicate with each other using their minds. Many, including Rex, could also communicate with animals. So, he always kept the animals he was carrying informed of where they were, and where they were going. They so appreciated what he said, that some tried to open the door to the cockpit. To thank him by licking him. One elephant stuck his trunk on top of his head, which shook him.

On another occasion he heard that a number of chickens were passing out because of the heat in Baghdad, Iraq. So, he flew out there and collected them, after first cooling the aircraft. So much so, that he and his fellow pilots had to wear sweaters. They loaded over 140,000 of them. Their feathers started to fill the plane. Then as they flew and began to land. The chickens asked Rex "Where are we going?'

"We are in Constanza" replied Rex. He arranged for someone to open the cargo door. All the chickens began talking to each other as they left the plane and headed for a nearby lake. Where a group of locals fed and cared for them.

Whenever Rex wasn't flying. He was usually caring for animals. He had farms in different parts of the world where he had herds of cows, and horses he enjoyed riding. He had a pet dog that he carried in his front basket on his yellow bike that he often cycled to a local coffee bar to meet with his friends. They couldn't resist stroking and feeding the dog. He was such a good organizer that he was often asked to help plan projects by communities. Then find solutions to any problem they experienced.

He also learnt to play a large baritone that no one else played. He was invited by Bing Bong the famous musician to join his brass band, that visited many towns. They marched for miles with thousands of people on either side of the road. The band then left in a large coach where they all began playing and singing. Rex always left his guitar and trumpet there which he also learned to play so he could join in with the other players as they returned to the Old Oak garden centre. He usually took his guitar into Bing Bongs jazz club where he watched many amazing jazz artists including Tony, that you can read about in the next chapter.

# VISITOR TWO-TONY THE JAZZ SINGER

A little boy arrived in The Plant World inside Bing Bong's recording studio. He sat in front of a microphone that was switched on. Bing Bong the musician had been recording a song he wrote. He had left the studio to get some food.

The little boy was curious as to where he was. He was wearing a pair of shorts and T-Shirt. He looked down at his legs and for some reason he began to sing the following chorus.

"Toe, Knee.

Hands and feet,

Let me walk

Down the street."

He began dancing around the room swinging his arms and legs. He stood in front of a piano and began pressing the keys. He was surprised at the different tones they made. He began singing the same chorus above, and added the following words using different tones.

"I can dance

I can play

I can sing,

loud and clear."

He didn't notice that Bing Bong had returned to the recording studio. He heard the boy singing and realized he was a new arrival. So, he sent a mental message to Uncle Twotrees to come over and see him, which of course he did. They both sat and watched him singing the above chorus, dancing around the room, and attempting to play the piano. Bing Bong recorded the song and broadcast it on his radio, and on the speakers outside the studio. Plant people passing bye were curious as to who was singing as he had such a wide range of voice. They couldn't resist dancing to his song which he kept adding more and different choruses. Uncle Twotrees entered the studio and introduced himself, He said out loud, in front of the microphone, that he will be called "Tony (Toe Knee) the Singer', as the slang name in the human world means, stylish." Uncle Twotrees knew he would become a very popular and stylish singer.

Tony heard the crowd outside cheering and applauding the new arrival. He went outside singing and dancing. The crowd were surprised how small he was but with such a powerful and lovely voice. They continued to cheer and applaud him. Much to Tony's delight.

Some children of his age which was five years asked if he would like to join their school choir. As you may know age and time is quite different than the human world. He said he would love to, but where is the school? The boy called Rapper Pablito suggested he stay at his house and then he would take him to the school the following morning. Tony agreed to go with him and as they both walked down the street. They both began singing. Mudanna who became a very famous singer followed them and joined in.

All three went to school together on the back of Gracious Peat's three-wheeler. They sang all the way and passers bye stopped, listened and cheered them. All three became members of the choir. Tony and Mudanna also became solo singers. Tony often visited Bing Bong's studio where he was taught how to play the piano. He also of course recorded more songs he had created that Bing Bong played on his radio station. Because his style of singing was unique, he became known as Tony The Jazz singer.

No one realized that he listened to the many dogs, cats and other animals he cared for. He tried singing the same notes as his pets, who loved the sound of his voice. As you may know in The Plant World, many Plant people can read the thoughts of animals. Tony did so. They also sang together.

The Video Queen made a video of him singing with his pets. It was called 'Meow, Meow, Woof, Woof.' She arranged with Fernando, known as Wiki. Who spent each day studying the human internet, to show the video on YouTube? Tony, became a popular singer on YouTube. Of course, humans didn't realize he was from a different dimension, who didn't visit them physically.

He not only cared for dogs and cats but also chameleons. They also loved his voice as it helped remove the stress they sometimes felt. Chameleons are in a class all of their own, and have unique characteristics like no other lizards. Tony began travelling and singing in other countries Wherever, he went he went searching for local chameleons. He was surprised to find so many different varieties, such as, Bearded Pygmy, Carpet, Crested, Four Horned, Green Pygmy, Panther. Rosette Nosed, Pitiless Pygmy chameleon. ( I suggest you visit this website that has pictures of all these chameleons, plus many others https://www.exotic-pets.co.uk/chameleons-for-sale.html. You should also watch the videos about Planet Wild organization that helps all living creatures. I enjoyed watching the video **https://youtube.be/ ZgltGjKu4mQ**

# VISITOR THREE-CALVIN -TRAVEL ORGANIZER

A young teenage boy with bald head arrived in Plant World sitting on a school desk at night with no one around him. He found a bench and slept on it. The following morning, he was surrounded by school children. One of them introduced himself and told him that he and many others were about to visit the countryside with Brown Owl the scout leader. He suggested he joins them, which he did. He climbed aboard a wagon that had two horses that took them into the countryside. He was amazed at what he saw and fascinated by what Brown Owl described. The journey took over 12 hours until they returned to the Old Oak Garden Center where everyone moved to their homes.

The teenage boy decided he wanted to explore the community and maybe visit other areas even at night. This he did for the next seven days and even reached the coastline where he found some boats including one managed by Wally. He asked him if he could sail with him. Wally asked what was his name. He didn't know and told him that. Ted realized he was a fairly new arrival so he took him to meet Uncle Twotrees who gives most new arrivals names, based on their character or future skill they will apply. He of course noticed he was bald and that he had unique non-conformist thoughts. Especially after he took him to another dimension to learn how to use his inner consciousness to mentally create amazing things. However, he decided to let him explore this dimension starting with Wally who was planning to sail around the world. He would meet with him later in his life. He decided to call him Calvin.

When Calvin returned to Wally's boat he climbed aboard and met Jessie who came with them. She was an artist and musician and taught Calvin how to play a piano and paint things. They went from continent to continent that are like the human world but more colourful and of course everyone cared and communicated with all the many varieties of animals. Calvin not only photographed the places and people he met but also wrote lots of pages describing the visit that included trips in land. On one occasion he landed in Canada and headed to Montreal. Whereas, Wally and Jessie told him they were going to the Caribbean and if he wanted them to come back and pick him up, they would do so if he sent a telepathic request to them.

Calvin enjoyed his visit to Montreal and stayed there for many years. Except when he visited other areas such as North and South America. Upon his return each time he promoted to everyone in Montreal about all the places he had visited and arranged tours for anyone who wanted to explore where he did. He had the most popular travel company, which of course didn't charge anyone to visit any location in the world. He met Rex the pilot who flew him to many continents that he arranged locals to travel with Rex.

He began to realize that there were so few places for his clients to live comfortably in when visiting overseas locations. He wished he could arrange to build free hotels but it would take so long in any location, especially to find locals with skills and equipment to build them. Uncle Twotrees tuned into him and came over to Montreal and suggested he joins him to visit another dimension, which he happily agreed to do. He took him to where Uncle Twotrees introduced him to a character called Seth who he was told is a teacher and educator that visits many dimensions.

"Welcome Calvin. You are in a dimension where your thoughts will seem to physically appear." Explained Seth.

"What can you see Calvin?" asked Uncle Twotrees.

Calvin looked around and was surprised at what he saw. Around Seth was a room full of books with his name on them. Around Uncle Twotrees, who was almost standing next to him, was a room full of lovely flowers and plants. The strange thing was that when Seth started to walk. The room and books remained around him. Even as he passed through the room full of plants. The books did not physically touch the flowers. They just floated through them as if they didn't exist. Then suddenly, the rooms disappeared and were replaced by different scenes of the countryside that Seth and Uncle Twotrees started to think about. Seth then suggested that Calvin thinks of a different scene.

To his utter amazement he began to mentally create a hotel which then appeared built in front of him. He actually mentally designed five different shapes and sizes that all immediately appeared in front of him, which he entered and thought of what the furniture would be like. Again, they all appeared in each room. Uncle Twotrees explained that he could use this inner consciousness to create things when he returned to Plant World

"How is this happening?' asked Calvin.

"Your physical brain is the mechanism by which thought or emotion is automatically formed into Electro-magnetic Energy (EE) units. The invisible EE units form your physical matter and represent the essential and basic units from which any physical particle appears. The EE units, are the psychic building blocks of matter. They are quite simply incipient forms of reality. Like seeds that are automatically given birth. They are suited for different environments. some appearing within the physical framework, and some not conforming at all to its prerequisites." Explained Seth

"In the dimension you are now in. Your thoughts will immediately appear. As the EE units move far faster than light and there are no physical barriers" Explained Uncle Twotrees.

"When I go back to the Plant world. Will I be able to use my thoughts to create things quickly that won't disappear? As it is happening here, as the hotel has disappeared? Asked Calvin.

Seth responded. "Yes, and if you ever enter the human world you can use your thoughts to create unbelievable things. Which, many humans do, but don't realize their thoughts become physical by the

EE units. I've written books for humans that have exercises in order to learn how to do so. As well as, understand the power of internal consciousness. Seth gave him a copy of "Seth Speaks' in which it explained about Electromagnetic Energy units that you can read about at the end of this chapter.

He returned to the Plant World Dimension where he read the book. He then spent almost all his time mentally creating different types of properties. Not only in Montreal, but also around the world after visiting a place with Rex the pilot. He had to make sure there was no one standing where his property was amazingly built in an instance. On one occasion he decided to visit The Dominican Republic to thank Wally and Jessie for moving him to Canada. Wally actually owned a free hotel in Sosua and was amazed at what Calvin explained what he had been doing. Wally told him he had a lovely piece of land next to a river and mountainside and was hoping to build a hotel there and a runway above the mountain. He took Calvin there who designed a hotel similar design to Wallys. He also created a long runway which he sent a mental message to Rex about, who flew over and landed there. Before climbing aboard the plane, he was introduced to some Sosua locals, such as, Eric who was planning to create an animal sanctuary and his mate Fernando known as WIKI who Calvin learnt he spoke Spanish and helped visitors communicate with locals. Calvin decided he would tell his clients who visited the Dominican Republic to make contact with him. He then met a lady called Cozette who was an interior designer who enjoyed teaching youngsters how to help others to build interior apartments. Calvin realized that he must invite her to help him mentally design hotel rooms and maybe tell her about EE units. So, he invited her to join him as he planned to fly with Rex to The Old Oak Garden Center in England, where Calvin taught students in the university how to create travel agencies and become tourist guides. They were all proud of what he taught them and described all the places he had visited. He also gave them the following article as it's a lot easier to learn how to apply it in Plant World Dimension.

# ELECTROMAGNETIC ENERGY (EE UNITS)

From Seth Speaks 'The Eternal Validity of the Soul' Chapter 20 Session 581© 1972 by Jane Roberts, © ???? by Robert F. Butts, © 2012 by Laurel Davies Butts Reprinted by permission of Amber-Allen Publishing, Inc., P.O. Box 6657, San Rafael, CA 94903. All rights reserved.

Robert F Butts explained the following which is in italics.

Four 4 people in attendance with Jane Roberts and Seth. Were asked to raise questions of Seth.

Question by M.H. Her query was based on a theory that, as it happened, I'd heard of also: A group of scientists has postulated the existence of a class of subatomic particles called "tachyons," or "meta-particles," that always travel faster than the speed of light. (According to the theory of relativity, no particle can be accelerated to the speed of light because its mass would become infinitely large as it approached light's velocity; but this barrier is bypassed by stating that the particles in question have an imaginary proper mass – not rest mass- that is never less than the speed of light. MH asked, then: "Are these faster-than-light particles the same as, or like, the electromagnetic energy or EE units Seth discusses in the Appendix of "The Seth Material", Seth replied: -

I told you some time ago that there were many gradations of matter, or form, that you do not perceive. In your terms many of these particles making up such constructions do move faster than the speed of your light.

Your light, again, represents only a portion of an even larger spectrum then that of which you know; and when your scientists study its properties, they can only investigate light as it intrudes into the three-dimensional system. The same of course applies to a study of the structure of matter or form.

There are indeed universes composed of such faster-than-light particles. Some of these in your terms share the same space as your own universe. You simply would not perceive such particles as mass. When these particles are slowed down sufficiently, you do experience them as matter.

Some of these particles drastically alter their velocity, appearing sometimes at your slower rate, usually in cyclic fashion. The inner vortex of some such particles has a much greater velocity than the orbiting portions. EE units are formed spontaneously from the electromagnetic reality of feelings emitted from each consciousness, as, for example, breath automatically goes from the physical body.

EE units are, then, emanations from consciousness. The intensity of the thought or emotion determines the characteristics of the units themselves. As certain ranges are reached, they are propelled into physical actualization. Whether or not this occurs in your terms they will exist as small matter particles – as, say, latent matter or pseudo matter.

Some of these will fall into the faster-than-light groupings, and have a perceivable vitality within that framework. These faster-than-light particles of course exist in their own kind of form then. There are many ranges and great varieties of such units, all existing beyond your perceivable reach. To lump them together in such a way, however, is misleading. For within all of this there is great order.

You are not utterly unaware of the existence of some of these units, though you do not experience them as mass. You interpret some of them as events, dream events, so-called hallucinations; and sometimes certain ranges of these units are interpreted by you as movement-through-time.

All of them cast certain "atmospheric conditions" or reflections that color physical events as you know them. Some of your own feelings are propelled into a reality within such systems, adopting within that framework their own mass and form. In the creation and maintenance of your normal reality, you focus your daily waking consciousness so that it becomes effective within the ranges necessary. Ideas and feelings that you want made physical carry within them the mechanisms that will put them in the proper range, well within the electromagnetic field necessary for physical development.

Your consciousness, however, is equipped to create realities in other fields as well. Now in certain dreams and out-of-body experiences. Your own consciousness moves faster than the speed of light, and under such conditions you are able to perceive some of these other forms of "mass or matter."

The EE units are quite simply incipient forms of reality: seeds automatically given birth, suited for different environments, some appearing within the physical framework, and some not conforming at all to its prerequisites. Now some systems of reality are "bounded" with centers of faster-than-light particles. These begin to slow down at a rhythmic rate toward the peripheries, in your terms over great distances, until actually the outside slower particles to some extent imprison the canter masses, even though they move much more quickly, but within a confined area.

The behaviors of such units, as you can now see, form the particular camouflage within the given system, while the peripheral activities effectively set up inner identities and outer boundaries. These are all variations, generally speaking and very simply put, on matter as you think of it. The same applies to negative or antimatter however, which you do not perceive in any case. But the gradations of activity within such systems are as diverse.

Basically, however, no system is closed. Energy flows freely from one to another, or rather permeates each. It is only the camouflage structure that gives the impression of closed systems, and the law of inertia does not apply. It appears to be a reality only within your own framework and because of your limited focus.

Now the duration and relative stability of such "matter" within other systems varies considerably, with intensity determining the strength of all such manifestations. The invisible EE units form your physical matter and represent the essential and basic units from which any physical particle appears.

It will not be physically perceived. You see only its results. Since consciousness can travel faster than the speed of light, then when it is not imprisoned by the slower particles of the body it can become aware of some of these other realities. Without training, however, it will not know how to interpret what it sees. The physical brain is the mechanism by which thought or emotion is automatically formed into EE units of the proper range and intensity to be used by the physical organism.

These EE units, then, are the psychic building blocks of matter.

# VISITOR FOUR -HUGH/ELIHU- CITY DESIGNER

A teenage boy arrived in Plant World holding a wooden stick. He looked down at his feet and found he was standing on acorns. For some reason he began picking them up, one at a time, and throwing it up in the air. Before it landed, he swung the stick and hit it. They began travelling further away and hitting various buildings, including greenhouses, surrounding 'The Old Oak Tree'.

A number of plant people working in the glass greenhouses were slightly shocked by the sound of the acorns. They came outside picked up the acorns and spotted the teenager with the stick. They walked slowly towards him, hoping not to be hit by an acorn. They then encircled him and began throwing the acorns at him. To their surprise he moved in all directions in order to hit the acorns up into the air. Other children passing by started to catch the acorns.

Uncle Twotrees who was sitting in the tree talking to Woo 'The Wise Old Owl' observed what was happening. To his surprise he saw the little boy hold up his hands and call out to everyone around him. To stop throwing and come over to talk to him, which they did.

He then began picking up other sticks lying on the ground. He then started to show everyone how to swing and hit the acorns. He then arranged for four groups to stand around Toot and practice throwing and hitting the acorns.

Uncle Twotrees sent a mind message to Widget the handyman to come over and watch what was happening. When he did so, he noticed that some of the sticks kept breaking after a while. Also, some children had difficulty holding them because they were quite thick and long. They eventually stopped playing and returned to the greenhouses to continue watering the plants.

Widget wandered over to the boy and they began discussing ways of making stronger and lighter sticks that children could handle. They then thought about what they could use to hit with it. Uncle Twotrees suggested they visit Dungo who collected rubbish from the plant and human worlds, and recycled everything.

Widget took him to Dungo's huge farm and sorted through tons of rubbish. They came across a ball made of cork and rubber, which is just what they were looking for. Widget then arranged with Dungo to find more rubber and cork and began making more balls. Meanwhile, the little boy wandered around the valley and came up with a design, on paper, of a stadium where they could hit and catch the ball, with spectators safely watching the players.

He gave the design to Uncle Twotrees who was surprised how detailed, and how huge the stadium was. He decided to call the boy 'Hugh' as he sensed he was going to have huge ideas. Which he did. He became an architect and designed, not only stadiums, but also many different types of buildings. He was invited from other countries to design and help build properties. Sandy, the house builder from Sosua in the Dominican Republic, invited him over to see the houses she had built. Sadly, he never met Calvin that mentally created properties.

He loved the scenery and warmth of the area. He especially liked seeing the ocean from the hills along the coastline. He thought about many plant people he had met in cold climates. He decided to create a city in Sosua, where they could come and enjoy the sunshine and explore the island. He met up with Wally who had a hotel in Sosua. They began working together to build the city.

He also met many other plant people, such as, Ted and Alan the cyclists who planned cycle trips inland for visitors. He also met Professor Dick the oceanographer and scientist. They worked together to build educational centers and trips by sea around the coast. Fernando, known as Wiki the computer expert that studied human websites, provided him with information about environmental locations in the human world.

In Plant world they don't have computers as they use their minds to communicate. But they enjoy watching videos, which is why Cerise, the Video Queen, is so popular. She began working with Hugh and his team in recording the development of the Sosua City. Uncle Twotrees, who visits humans in their dreams realized that the Jewish community would enjoy living in the city. He suggested to Hugh that he creates a web site and adds Video Queens video to it, on the human internet. They called it Sosua75.

Hugh became very famous in the plant world not only for all the baseball grounds he built. But also, for the amazing Sosua city, that attracted plant people from all over the world. They so enjoyed the physical and mental experience. Of course, he built a baseball and sports stadium in his city, that became the canter for world competitions. Some residents called him mayor, others president.

# . VISITOR FIVE-CERISE-INTERVIEWER

A young girl found herself sitting under a table covered by a table cloth. When she entered Plant World. Around her were four pairs of shoes. She then heard the four talking to each other. She, wasn't sure who they were so she kept quiet and they never knew she was sitting there.

She listened to every word that was spoken, which she found interesting. As it gave her a mental picture of each speaker. When, they left the table, she stuck her head out to see what they looked like. She also, checked that no one at another table spotted her. She stayed there for the rest of the day, until everyone left. She then stood up and wandered to the kitchen, were she found lots of food that she began eating. There was also, a couch in the corner of the main room, which she slept on. Then the following morning when she heard someone unlocking the door. She ran and hid under the table. Once again, she listened to every word spoken for the whole of the day and evening.

She was so interested in what everyone was talking about. That she started to write on the back of various pieces of paper she found. What stories they had been talking about. As she started to grow taller, she could no longer hide under the table. So, she actually, asked to join various groups of people at coffee tables. She became very popular as she had so many stories that interested people. She of course continued to note down what she heard.

One night while relaxing in bed. She started to communicate with spiritual guides from another dimension that visit the human world, as well as the Dream world. They started to tell her about people she met that she was talking with. This at first surprised her as she was able to see what their future lives would be. So, she began privately to tell them what her guides in her inner soul were telling her. She even wrote a life coaching book called URBAN PROVERBS that Fernando arranged for it to be published in the human world.

Then one day she met for coffee with the Video Queen who suggested she start making videos about the things she heard and learnt that would help dream children explore and experience the Plant World.

A number of senior plant people often gave lectures but Cerise did so in a different way. She arranged with many musicians and singers, such as Tony the jazz singer, to entertain her visitors, especially those sent by Calvin. She also enjoyed listening and dancing with everyone. Afterwards they all settled down and listened to what she had to tell them about Plant World, as well as, life coaching in the human world, where they had originally come from before dreaming and visiting Plant World.

What she didn't realize is that the Video Queen, with the help of Fernando, known as Wiki. Downloaded her video stories about the human world on to the human YouTube site. They too became very popular.

# VISITOR SIX- SHIRA THE YOGA TEACHER

A little girl found herself in a storeroom that was full of items covering the floor, and some reaching the ceiling. She struggled to reach the floor from her bed that was stacked upon ten others. She had to grab hold of each mattress that strengthened her wrists.

On the floor she didn't know which direction to head for as there were a number of narrow spaces between objects. She began to sing.

"Which way shall I go?

This way, that way,

Or climb up there.

Or should I walk?

Or climb up those stairs?

Or walk over to that door.

Over there?"

She found herself twisting and turning, stretching and kneeling until eventually she reached the door, which she opened. She found herself in a small room with sink, cooker, and refrigerator that contained lots of healthy foods and drinks, that she began eating and drinking.

Afterwards, she went back into the room that she realized was a great place for doing exercises. She began climbing up cupboards then jumping from one to the other. On one occasion she jumped down onto a bed and found herself bouncing onto the next bed. Something, she enjoyed doing every day. She reached the highest point in the room and began singing loudly.

"I'm a pretty girl,

I love to sing and dance.

I can twist and turn,

Climb and jump.

Over every lump."

Uncle Twotrees heard her voice, as he passed the building and crept inside. He watched her leaping from object to object. Twisting and turning along narrow corridors while singing. She eventually spotted him and came over to say "Hello"

"Welcome to Plant World young lady who I'll name you as Shira" replied Uncle Twotrees.

"Why" asked Shira.

"Because in the human world, Shira is a Hebrew feminine given name meaning 'poetry', 'singing' or 'music'. The Latin spelling of the Arabic name means 'beautiful'. Plus, you have the looks of an Indian. So, I assume your parents in India dreamed about you being very talented.

As I can see into the future. I know that you will become a yoga expert. You will then begin to travel the world teaching everyone how to become fit and healthy. You will also develop a skill at looking into individual's future lives. I suggest I take you round to Stella the clairvoyant." Which he did.

Stella taught her how to read Tarot cards and explain the possibilities of individuals future lives. While in The Old Oak canter in England. She not only gave plant people tarot readings, but she also advised them how to develop new skills to help others. Which is what everyone in Plant World does.

She also met Dr Wiggly who taught her how to stretch all her muscles without any pain. He happened to mention that Wally was planning to sail to India to explore the land. He suggested she went with him, as there are lots of talented Yoga teachers there.

Wally was happy to take her along, as he was accompanied by his friend Jessie Agnes, who was also a sailor, an artist, and musician. They had a wonderful trip as Wally had placed a piano onboard. Shira and Jessie created many songs that Wally loved listening to. On arrival in India they all went exploring together, until Shira met a remarkable

Yoga teacher. She trained him for many months. While Wally and Agnes left India to explore other countries, such as, islands in the Caribbean.

In plant world almost everyone can read each other's thoughts. They can also send mental messages thousands of miles away. Wally, sent one to Shira after he landed in the Dominican Republic which he found so beautiful.

Shira, decided to visit him, and sent out a global message. "Is anyone travelling from India to the Dominican Republic?" Ted the cyclist and yachtsman picked up the message. He arranged to pick her up in India and take her to a town called Cabarete, with miles of sandy beach. She loved the atmosphere and stayed there where she began teaching the locals yoga, as well as, giving them tarot readings, which they found fascinating.

# VISITOR SEVEN -CORRINE THE MOTORCYCLIST.

A little girl arrived in Plant World sitting in a warehouse in a United States city called Bend. In most countries everyone preferred to cycle or ride horses to get around. In the USA motorbikes were popular as they had so much more land to explore. Like the rest of Plant world there is no such thing as money. Things were designed and built for free because it is what someone wanted. Farmers grew things and gave their food away, while locals helped them to build trenches, and buildings. Or do anything they may need.

The warehouse was full of motorbikes, helmets, jackets, gloves and other articles of clothing. In the middle of the warehouse was a large ring where riders could try riding different bikes. The little girl couldn't resist sitting on different bikes, until she learnt how to start one of them. She suddenly found herself racing towards a wall, but she found the brake, and stopped just in time.

She then slowly accelerated and moved the bike around the track. She then started to ride many other bikes. What she enjoyed was the sound of the revving engine. The loudest was a bike called Harley Davidson. She didn't know that the builders had contacted WIKI the internet expert to ask him how to build bikes from the human world. He sent them loads of information. He even arranged for Dungo, who secretly visited the human world to collect things that Plant People would enjoy seeing, or having. He came to Bend on one occasion with a cartload of motorbikes that they copied and distributed around the USA.

Uncle Twotrees occasionally visited Bend to make sure the motorcyclists were not hurting or disturbing the wild life. He happened to be there when the little girl arrived. He heard her revving up many bikes. He went inside the warehouse, through the main large door, to see what was going on. He spotted the little girl and decided to call her Corrinne as the word sounds like a revving bike COR INN. The name also means maiden which of course she was.

Corinne saw the open door and immediately headed outside. She was amazed to see a wide track headed up towards a mountain side. She, went hurtling up it but she was not wearing any protective gear. Uncle Twotrees turned to the owner of the warehouse, called Jefa, and asked her to go after her and bring her back.

This she did, but she was surprised how fast Corinne was travelling. She came alongside her and told her to stop, which she did. They then returned slowly to the warehouse. Where many plant people, on bikes, were waiting to greet her. She noticed that they were all wearing helmets and special clothing. They all became friends and often went travelling together showing Corinne some beautiful spots in the countryside.

On one occasion she was travelling alone when she noticed a farm yard with horses and a number of different style wagons that the horses pulled. She spotted a lady busy building a new wagon. She went over and introduced herself. The lady was pleased to meet her. She was called Wainer. She showed her what she was building. Corinne suddenly had an idea and asked her if she would come with her to the warehouse. She wandered over to a lovely looking stallion and harnessed him to a very fast looking cart. She then followed Corinne to the warehouse, where they met Jefa.

Corinne rushed over to her and told her what Wainer was building. She wondered if she could build something that could be attached to motorbikes that could be used to carry things and maybe friends. Jefa took Wainer around the warehouse, showing her all the bikes. She told her what Corinne had suggested. Wainer suggested building a sidecar, which Jefa organized.

While the first one was being built. Corinne had begun sorting through all the clothing in the warehouse. Being creative, she began designing many different styles that became very popular. So much so, that Kiki the fashion designer added them to all his fashion shops around Plant world. He also, arranged with Dungo to drop off samples to various motorcycle shops in the Human world. He also asked WIKI to create a web site listing all of Corinne's designs.

Thousands of motorcyclists in the human world started to contact the web site, ordering many items. With the help of WIKI and Gazelle the executive's assistant. Corinne, opened a bank account in the human world. She then arranged for the money to be given to humans that were protecting animals, birds, bees and all living things. Kiki, arranged for all the items to be made and delivered in the human world.

Although Corinne was fairly busy. She still spent time riding and exploring the countryside with her friends.

# VISITOR EIGHT- MICHELE FOLK ARTIST AND COOK

A little girl arrived in Plant World and found herself alone in a large greenhouse full of beautiful flowers. She started to wander around and came across some large notebooks with empty pages, and alongside where a number of colored crayons. She picked them up and sat on a table and started to draw the plants around her, but they weren't exact replicas of the plants. She had a style whereby she added faces to each plant and flower. She even added hats, sun glasses, scarves and other items that personalized each plant.

Her art form was known as Folk Art. What surprised her was that some of the flowers that she was drawing. Started to tell he in her mind that they loved what she was doing. Some even told her their names.

It was many months later, when she attended The Old Oak Garden school. That she learnt that plant people communicated with each other using their minds. Also, some plant people communicated with animals, but not so many with plants, which they spent their time caring for. There is no violence or anger in Plant World as everyone is so busy. looking to help all living things.

Michele, started to draw pictures on the plant pots that were very colorful. The following morning Uncle Twotrees visited the greenhouse with many other plant people. They planned to collect the latest flowers and take them to The Old Oak Garden Centre' in the human world. As they were running short of plants to sell following their open day.

They stood back in complete wonder as they spotted all the colorful plant pots and above them paintings of the plant. They then spotted Michele in the corner looking out the window and drawing a picture of The Old Oak tree.

Uncle Twotrees sent a mind message to the famous chef Delia Urn. He asked her to bring some food for the little girl, which she immediately did so. Michele not only ate the food but she also studied every piece and asked Delia how did she make it.

Delia decided she should teach the little girl how to cook. So, she took her back to her place above her restaurant. She never stopped asking questions and couldn't resist experimenting with all kinds of food.

She was particularly clever at baking cakes that she took to school with her. Where both the teachers and students queued to try her latest cake.

The teachers asked her if she would provide meals for the cricket team when playing against other teams. She did so, but soon realized she needed to make at least twice as much food. As, spectators kept creeping into the pavilion and eating her food and cakes. Many also came to see her colorful designs she added to the cakes, including the faces of each cricket player.

She left school at an early age as there was such a demand for her food, as well as, all the paintings of plants and plant pots. Being a Folk artist, she started creating many other objects using natural materials, such as, wood, leaves, seeds, and stones, Not only where they popular around Plant World. But more so in the human world and were known as Michele Art. Peter the owner of the Old Oak Garden Centre was often asked by high end magazines, where Michele lived so that they could interview her,

Peter hinted that she lived in the Caribbean as Michele started to create faces and shapes of coconuts. Sandy the builder in the Dominican Republic sent them to Widget. He then arranged with Dungo to carry them over to the human world.

Dean Charles, Walter, Jessica and Crazy Ted in Plant World brought them over from the Caribbean to England on their boats each month. Along with other Caribbean materials that Michele used to create new forms of folk art.

As she grew older, she started to sail back with the boat owners who dropped her off in various countries in order to find new materials to add to her Folk Art. The plant people in many countries created show rooms so that her designs could be shown to the population in that country. She was the most famous Folk artist in Plant World.

# VISITOR NINE-ALIA THE DOG TRAINER

A little girl arrived in Plant World laying in a dog kennel with two dogs who started licking her face and hands. She didn't know what was happening until she opened her eyes. One of the dogs, a bull terrier held out his paw which the girl held and shook. The other dog, a golden Labrador, started licking her bare feet that made her giggle. She then began stroking their backs with both hands. They both then laid on their backs so that she could stroke their tummy. That she enjoyed doing. They then cuddled up to her and all three fell fast asleep.

She wasn't aware it was night time. Until, she heard other dogs barking outside the kennel around 6am. She stuck her head out the door where to her surprise she saw over twenty different type dogs. They all came over to say hello. She stood up and went and stroked each one. Somehow, she mentally knew the name of each one and sensed they were communicating with her. Using their minds and images of what they wanted to tell her.

One of the dogs had a collar and lead that he grabbed in his teeth and handed it to her. He then started to take her past loads of kennels towards a house in the corner. As she neared it she began to notice a strange smell. That was because the house belonged to Dungo the smelliest person in Plant World. He collected rubbish and recycled it each day. Plus, he stored manure in his back yard. Although he smelt badly, he was liked by all plant people because he cared for all animals. (That you can read about in my book 'The Secret World of the Plant People' Chapter thirteen).

"Hello little girl. Have you just arrived in Plant World?" asked Dungo.

"Yes, I think so. Are these your dogs?" asked the girl.

"Yes. Plus, I have many animals I care for, such as cats, shire horses, llamas, goats, chimpanzee, elephant. Would you like me to show you them?

"Oh Yes please. I so enjoyed meeting your dogs. May I continue to sleep with them in their kennels?"

"Yes. I'll make you a camp bed that you can sleep on."

"Thank you. Please make sure its large enough for the dogs to lay with me,"

Dungo then started to show her around his huge farm. He first showed her the new stables next to his house. They had been rebuilt by the plant people after they caught fire. The horses were rescued by The Three Heroes who you can see on the cover of my book, 'The Secret World of Dream Animals and Plants'.

Every animal she met she went up to it. Said hello and stroked it. She noticed some of the animals didn't look healthy. She asked Dungo to leave her with the animal that she began to hug and used her hands to heal the animal. Dungo, was very impressed at she was doing, as that is exactly what he did. But he began doing it when he was an adult. He was surprised that such a young girl had the healing abilities. He sent a mental message to Uncle Twotrees. Telling him there was a new arrival at his farm.

Uncle Twotrees came over and followed them both. Watching how she communicated with all the animals she met, and how she so enjoyed healing some of them.

"Hello young girl. You are very beautiful and in a state of extreme happiness when with animals. I sense you are going to be very noble and supreme personality. Which is why I will call you ALIA that in the human world means someone who is sublime, exalted, noble and supreme.

Alia spent every day visiting all the animals on Dungo's farm. On an evening she stood in the middle of all the dog kennels and started to teach them how to develop their individual skills. In plant world all animals care for each other, as they can read each other's thoughts, and those of plant people. So, they don't naturally chase the cats that lived next door.

She started to go to school accompanied by many of the dogs, who enjoyed being with her. She then introduced each dog to different schoolmates and taught them how to care for and play with the dogs. Individual dogs then began leaving the school with the new child. But they always returned the following day so that they could play with Alia at playtime.

Breeze who had three dogs called Mercedes, Porche and Karma also had a dog training school. Where she met Petra and her newfoundland dogs. Together they started a Dog show where pet owners competed with each other. They also, travelled to other countries looking for homeless dogs that they found homes for. They heard about Alia and asked her to join them in creating more dog schools in different countries, such as the Dominican Republic.

She so liked the environment that she stayed there in a town called Cabarete. Where she not only had a dog school. But she was always wandering around looking for any animal that needed company and help. As you may know. Every Plant person cares for all animals. But sometimes animals went exploring the island, and injured themselves falling down mountain sides, or floating in the ocean or rivers. She met Eric the animal rescuer who looked after all stray animals, before finding someone to care for each one. She also rescued animals that she communicated with for reasons explained below.

# ANIMALS HAVE CONSCIOUSNESS.

I've copied this from. From 'Dreams, "Evolution," and Value Fulfilment', Volume 1 © 1986 by Jane Roberts, © 1997 by Robert F. Butts, © 2012 by Laurel Davies Butts Reprinted by permission of Amber-Allen Publishing, Inc., P.O. Box 6657, San Rafael, CA 94903. All rights reserved.

The text in italics are comments by the medium Jane Roberts who Seth took over and explained everything to her husband Robert F Butts who wrote everything he said.

Earlier that day I'd made a wadded-up paper ball for Mitzi to play with. Using her lightning-quick reflexes, she kept knocking it around the living room and beneath Jane's rocker as my wife went into trance, then began to speak. Her littermate, Billy, is to be neutered early next year. I mentioned the guilt Jane and I feel because we're depriving the cats of their reproductive roles in life, and because we don't let them run free in the environment. Here are session excerpts

Good evening.

("Good evening, Seth.")

Observing the antics of your Mitzi gives me an excuse to begin the topic of the evening: animal consciousness. I want to begin simply by having you question some concepts taken quite for granted-to question much.

It is somewhat fashionable to see man as always nature's despoiler, as the destructive member of nature's family, or even to consider him apart from nature, who was given nature as his living grounds. It is somewhat fashionable to see man as ... the creature who dirties his own nest, and I am not condoning much of man's behaviour in that regard.

However, there are other issues, and questions seldom asked. You ignore the fact that [overall] the consciousness of animals has its own purposes and intents. It is true that animals are slaughtered under the most cruel of circumstances for human consumption—for then they are treated simply as foodstuff.

Buffaloes do not roam as they did before. There are thousands of farm-bred animals, however [and have been], all throughout civilization, alive for a time, well-cared-for for a time-animals who in usual terms would not exist except for man's "gluttonous" appetite for meat. That is the way the issue is often considered

It seldom occurs to anyone that certain forms of animal consciousness came in physical form [by choice], that certain species are prized by man and protected, or that the consciousnesses of such animals had anything at all to do with such an [overall] arrangement.

You cannot say that such animals came out ahead of the bargain, but you can say that the species of man and certain species of animals together formed an arrangement. . . that did have benefits for both. Man is more a part of nature than he realizes, and in the greater realm of activity he cannot take any... actions with which the rest of nature does not agree for its own reasons.

Remember here other material given about cellular communication, for example, and the vast web of intercommunication that unites all species. Of course, animals can communicate with man, and of course man can communicate with other species— with all species. Such communication has always gone on. Man cannot afford to become aware of such communication at this point, simply because your entire culture is based upon the idea of the animals' "natural" subordinate position. The men who slaughter animals cannot afford to treat those animals as possessors of living consciousnesses.

There is, beneath it all, an important unity, a sense of communion, as one portion of earth's living consciousness dies to insure the continued life of all nature. That natural sacrament, however, turns into something else entirely when the gift is so misunderstood, and when the donor is treated so poorly.

Basically, (many farmers love) animals for themselves, and delight in their ways- but by itself "delighting in animals" is not considered particularly virile enough. In your society, if you like animals you must not like them for themselves, but for other reasons.

If you want to be with animals then you must become a farmer, or a veterinarian, or a cattleman, or whatever.

Many animals enjoy work and purpose. They enjoy working with man. Horses enjoyed the contributions they made to man's world. They understood their riders far more than their riders understood them. Many dogs enjoy being family protectors. There are deep emotional bonds between men and many species of animals. There is emotional response. Dolphins, for example, respond emotionally to man's world. The animals on a farm are emotionally aware of the overall psychological content of the farmer's life and, (that of each member), of his family.

Consciousness is filled with content—any kind of consciousness. (The farmer's) animals understand that in a certain fashion he is a midwife, responsible for some of their births. Food comes from his hands. The animals understand, on their own, that life on any terms that are physical ends with death—that the physical properties must be returned to the earth from which they came.

(Animals), do not blame (human beings) for anything. If as a species you really found yourselves communicating with the animals, you would have an entirely different culture, a culture that would indeed bring about an alteration of consciousness of the most profound nature.

You have forgotten, conveniently, how much you learned from all of the animals, as I have mentioned in past sessions. You learned a good deal of medicine from watching animal behaviour. You learned what plants to avoid, and which to cultivate. You learned how to rid yourself of lice by going into the water. You learned social behaviour by watching the animals.

At one time you could identify with animals, and they with you to a remarkable degree. They have been your teachers, though they did not choose your path. Obviously, you could not have gone your way, (as a species), had it not been for the animals.

Domesticated animals have their own reasons for choosing such a state. It is, for example, usual enough to think that your cats (Billy and Mitzi) should ideally run outside in the open, because in the wild that is what cats would do.

Cats in the wild were, in those terms of time, exploring one kind of nature. In that kind of nature, with a natural population taken care of in the environment, there would be far fewer cats than there are now. Your cats would not exist. Why does it seem antinatural, even slightly perverse, for a household cat to, say, prefer fine cat food from a can, when it seems that he should be eating mice, perhaps, or dining upon grasshoppers?

The household cat is exploring a different kind of nature, in which he has a certain relationship to human consciousness, a relationship that changes the reality of his particular kind of consciousness.

Your cats are as alive in all ways inside of the house as out. They understand their relationship with your human reality. They enjoy contributing in your life as much as any wild animal enjoys being a part of its group. Their consciousnesses lean in a new direction, feel about the edges of concepts, sense openings of awareness of a different kind, and form alliances of consciousness quite as natural as any other.

There is no such things as a cat consciousness, basically speaking, or a bird consciousness. In those terms, there are instead simply consciousnesses, that choose to take certain focuses.

NOTE. Session 906 on Viruses and how our feelings can affect our animals.

Seth first mentioned viruses in the 17th session for January 26, 1964, when I asked him to comment upon the recent deaths of our dog, Mischa, at the age of 11, and of a pair of kittens Jane had obtained from the janitor of the art gallery where she worked part time. (The kittens had the same mother, but had come from successive litters.) I was 44 and Jane was 34, and in conventional terms both of us were still struggling- not only to learn about ourselves and the world, but to find our creative ways in that world. Seth's answer to my question was more than a little surprising and saddening to us, and opened up a number of insights:

The particular atmosphere surrounding your personalities just prior to the animals' deaths were destructive, short-circuited, and filled with inner panics. I do not want to hurt your feelings. That is, I am sorry to say, a natural occurrence on your plane. The fact is that the animals caught your emotional contagion, and according to their lesser abilities translated it for themselves.

The viruses and infections were of course present. They always are. They are themselves fragments, struggling small fragments without intention of harm. You have general immunity, believe it or not, to all such viruses and infections. Ideally, you can inhabit a plane with them without fear. It is only when you give tacit agreement that harm is inflicted upon you by these fragments. To some degree, lesser, dependent lives such as household pets are dependent upon your psychic strength. They have their own, it is true, but unknowingly you reinforce their energy and health.

When your own personalities are more or less in balance, you have no trouble at all in looking out for these creatures, and actually reinforcing their own existence with residues of your creative and sympathetic powers. In times of psychological stress or crisis, quite unwittingly you withhold this strong reinforcement.

In the cats' deaths, both cats inherited the peculiar illness, which was a virus, that killed them. In the case of the first cat, you were able to reinforce its strength and maintain its health for quite a while, and then you needed your energies for yourselves. The second cat barely enjoyed such reinforcement at all, and quickly succumbed.

Your dog's illness was incipient. You could not have maintained his health for many long years in any case. I would like to make clear, of course, that animals certainly do have energy to maintain their own health, but this is strongly reinforced as a rule by the vitality of human beings to whom the animals are emotionally attached. The fact is, you were not able to give your dog that added emotional vitality at a time when he needed it most. There is no need to blame yourselves. It was beyond your control. "

Animals, like people, sense when they are a burden, and the dog sensed that he was a burden, and also something of a nuisance. I would have preferred that you did not ask me this question, but since you did, and since you both loved the dog, it deserves an answer."

Mischa, who was part shelty, or Shetland collie, was the last dog we've had. He certainly was a true companion to us. Even now, as I write about him over 16 years later, I feel a strong emotional pull toward him.

# VISITOR TEN - ELIZABETH THE DENTIST

A young married couple spent most of their days working but, on a night, they slept and dreamt. The husband who was a dentist started to dream of having a child.

That child appeared in the Secret World of the Plant People. Where dream children began immediately developing their skills and talents. Everyone in the Plant World care for all living things They also learn how to read each other's thoughts and often use telepathy to communicate not only with other plant people but also, with animals, birds, bees, and some with plants and trees.

Uncle Twotrees tries to meet all new arrivals to give them a name based on their skills and future role.

When he saw this little girl, he tuned into the dreamer, and realized that he was going to call his daughter Elizabeth. So, that is what he called her in Plant World.

Elizabeth arrived in a studio full of paintings and found a blank one on an easel surrounded by brushes and paints. She immediately started to experiment and began copying some of the paintings. Stella whose studio it belonged to. Met her and gave her a large sketch book and pencils and taught her how to draw things she saw.

She couldn't wait to wake up and start exploring the countryside where she started drawing all the plants, trees, birds and insects she found. She didn't know then, that the birds and insects knew what she was doing so they sat still until she had an accurate drawing of them.

One evening she was passing Bing Bongs Club where they played different types of music in different dance floors on many floors. She entered the club and found herself dancing as she listened to the bands playing. She moved up to each floor and joined in. She learnt how to jive, twist, waltz, quick step, and then on the top floor the music was completely different and the walls were covered in mirrors. She sat and watched young girls moving all parts of their body in tune to the music. She eventually joined them every day and became a popular ballerina.

She learnt many skills as she grew older. Then one day she felt a desire how to help some of her friends who had broken their teeth. Little did she know that her other self in the human world had become a dentist and her thoughts and skills were picked up by her. Because in plant world everyone eats healthy foods, drink plenty of water, always breathing deeply, and exercise regularly. So, very few who have teeth problems.

# VISITOR ELEVEN-PING PONG

A little boy arrived in Plant World sitting on a branch of an almond tree overlooking a muddy river. He started collecting the almonds then began throwing them as far as he could. He noticed that when they hit something, they made a sound 'Ping' or 'Splosh' when they landed in the river below.

He started to climb down the tree when he suddenly slipped and fell into the muddy bank. He climbed out covered in mud, but he noticed all the stones lying on the ground and started throwing them and listening to all the sounds they made.

He suddenly stopped when from behind a bush he heard someone shout 'Ow' when a stone hit him. It was Uncle Twotrees who wandered over to the little boy and told him he had to be careful when throwing stones as it may hurt someone or break something.

The little boy apologized and asked him where he was.

Uncle Twotrees told him he was in Plant World and that over the hill he pointed to was The Old Oak Garden Centre. All of a sudden, a group of children appeared who were being shown the countryside by Brown Owl the brownie leader. She wandered over and as she grew closer held her nose as the little boy was very smelly as he was covered in mud from the river where many animals drank and pooed.

She asked Uncle Twotrees what his name was and he replied 'Ping Pong'. She then escorted the boy to a nearby waterfall and with the help of the children washed him and his clothes. Fortunately, some of the children had extra items of clothing in their haversacks and gave them to Ping Pong.

They then all returned to their campsite where they cooked Ping Pong a meal before they all slept in their tents. Ping Pong was so happy to be with all these children who spent the night telling him all about the Plant world.

In the morning he had fun exploring the area with his new friends. They played hide and seek, climbed trees, where they swung on ropes from one tree to another, and went zip lining across a stream.

There was a lot to do as Widget the handyman had built tree houses and connecting walkways. While, Warren built tunnels for them to hide in and explore. Dribbles the footballer built a sports area that included a football field, a volley ball court, and table tennis tables.

Ping Pong picked up a bat and started to hit the ball against a wall. He liked the sound and found the ball returned to his feet after hitting the wall. Dribbles taught him how to play and was amazed how quickly he learnt. He was so good that no one could beat him but they enjoyed playing with him as they had such long rallies.

He became an expert at whatever he was taught to do at the campsite. He had such fun playing with everyone that he stayed at the campsite, except for occasional visits to The Old Oak Garden Centre. On one occasion he met Crazy Ted the cyclist who taught him how to ride. Then Widget gave him a bicycle that he rode back to the campsite.

He then started to build a series of race tracks with the help of Alan the cyclist and builder. Some of the tracks went up the sides and top of hills. Crazy Ted joined them and all three tested every track to make sure they were safe even though some where quite challenging. The three of them had loads of fun racing each other.

While they built the tracks, Widget started building off road racing bikes that Dungo took to the campsite on the back of his wagon pulled by his favorite shire horses.

Children from all over England and from abroad came to the campsite to meet Ping Pong who was now in charge of the campsite. He taught them everything he knew, especially how to ride bikes up and down hills. They had such fun that the children from abroad asked him if he could come to their country and create a campsite, which he did. He spent decades travelling and building adventure play grounds.

He even went as far as the Dominican Republic in the Caribbean where it was very hot so he built playgrounds next to the ocean so the children could cool off in the sea. He liked the island so much that he spent most of his time there. He just relaxed after many years building adventure play grounds.

# VISITOR TWEVE-ACTION-FILM MAKER

I will explain later in this story as to why this little boy was called Action.

He woke up in Plant World to find himself surrounded by cameras, video equipment and a tv camera. He didn't know what they were used for but like all Dream children entering Plant world he was curious. He found a machine that when he pressed various buttons showed moving pictures on a screen. It was called an editing machine whereby film makers take out and stick together different bits of film. Every film you see in the cinema has been edited by experts and you would never know it. Sadly, in the human world some editors put different pictures together that have nothing to do with the story. For example, two leaders shaking hands that may never had met.

No one in Plant World would ever dream of doing something like that, as it's dishonest. What you see is what you get WYSIWYG as no one tries to hide anything which is not surprising as Plant people can read each other's thoughts.

The little boy spent days working out what each piece of equipment did. Then one day he left the studio carrying a video camera on one shoulder and started filming everything he saw. He happened to stop Widget as he was about to climb on his famous bike. He asked him if could go with him and film what he was doing.

"Of course, replied Widget jump on the back."

Which he did and as he climbed aboard, he called out to Widget "Okay, Action."

"What do you mean 'Action' asked a puzzled Widget?

"It's what film directors say when they start filming" replied the little boy. He kept jumping off the bike to film different shots of

Widget. He of course used the word quite often that day. So much so that Widget nicknamed him Action.

At the end of each day he placed the film in the editing machine and cut out the bits of him jumping off the bike as that wasn't interesting to anyone who may watch his first film. Everyone, in the Garden centre soon got used to being filmed. Action had a knack of capturing on film the unusual and often funny events. That is why everyone wanted to see his next tv program and film.

He expanded the studio, with the help of Widget, to include a film studio, and a cinema. Where he mostly showed films that made Plant people laugh. As he grew older, he added other bits to his cinema including a classroom where he taught students at the Old Oak Academy how to create film and write scripts. It was one of the most popular courses in the university that attracted students from all over Plant World. Many came just to meet Action whose music videos were watched by every teenager. Mudanna, the famous singer, always got Action and Bing Bong, the musician, to make all her videos.

Action always looked forward to making the next Mudanna video. As she was such fun and always doing naughty things that her fans loved. He always took two crews. One to film the music video and the other to video the other team videoing Mudanna and following her to see what she got up to. Older plant people watched both but preferred to see in a cinema what Mudanna got up to. So that they could "tut, tut" to each other and talk about what she got up to, for days.

I will tell you about the last video in a future story about Action.

# VISITOR THIRTEEN-HIKER

A little boy arrived in Plant World sitting on a small rock surrounded by trees. He stood up and began making his way up a small hillside. Every time, he saw a different tree, plant, or flower. He would stop and study it. He held a tree trunk in his arms and was surprised when he heard a voice in his mind say," Hello young boy."

When he spotted a new flower, he would kneel down, smell and stroke it. Other plants he would study them, such as, counting the number of leaves and berries. Which he sometimes ate when hungry. He had to be careful as some plants, such as, toadstools. Gave him stomach ache.

He also, stopped on many occasions to watch and study birds sitting on branches. Before flying away. On one occasion while studying them, a rabbit came and sat on his lap. He couldn't resist stroking it, as well as, talking to it. Again, he heard a voice in his mind saying "Thank you for tickling my back."

If he spotted a narrow path. He couldn't resist walking along it and exploring everything on either side. He went along, one path that ended at a gate, which he opened. He found himself surrounded by huge horses. One of them suggested he climb on his back. Which he did. He was then led to a house, next to a stable. Where he met Dungo who cared for all animals, and recycled waste products.

"Hello. Have you just arrived in Plant World?" asked Dungo.

"Yes Sir. The plants in this world are amazing" said the little boy.

Dungo sent a mental message to Uncle Twotrees who soon came over to meet the new arrival. He asked him where he arrived. The boy told him about the rock, and then how he had fun exploring the countryside. Uncle Twotrees told him that he will be called 'Hiker' as he foresaw him walking and exploring all parts of the world.

This is exactly, what he did as he grew older. He became an expert of all living things in the countryside, in many different continents. He was also, invited to give lectures to students in The Old Oak University. His lectures were unique, as they left the classroom and went exploring the countryside to learn about every plant.

Plant people of all ages accompanied him when he went exploring. Even, Gordon Zola the cheese expert, went with him. When he visited the north coast of the Dominican Republic. He was so fascinated by what he was shown. That he decided to encourage local children to visit a piece of land he discovered. That had a large variety of trees and plants. He also added donkeys, guinea pigs, goats, ducks, fishes and birds that enjoyed roaming the area. It became so popular, that visitors to the island arriving on boats, came over to learn about every Dominican plant. As well, as, to stroke the animals and view the beautiful countryside. It was called Taino Valley Tropical Park.

Hiker inspired many others to create parks around the world. While in the Dominican Republic he couldn't resist exploring the sandy beaches on the coastline. He started to swim in the warm ocean but wanted to see what was below the ocean. He met Jürgen who taught people how to dive using diving equipment. They became friends and went exploring all over the coastline.

He was amazed at the scenery in the ocean, as well as, the large variety of sea animals. It reminded him of how he emotionally felt. When he started to explore the countryside as a small boy. Once again, he became an expert about everything he saw in the ocean, which he described to locals and visitors.

I hope you will begin exploring the countryside with your family and friends. If possible, take a black plastic bag with you, to remove any rubbish you find that may harm animals, or birds. As you grow older you may want to learn to scuba dive to explore your local sea.

# VISITOR FOURTEEN- YUVELIS- HEALER

Yuvelis arrived in Plant World and found she was sitting on a hay stack surrounded by lots of farm animals. They were all looking at her, curious to know where she suddenly came from, as she wasn't there while they were eating the hay that morning.

"Hello. Could you please tell me where I am?" asked Yuvelis with her voice

She did not realize that animals don't understand Plant People unless they use their mind to paint pictures of what they are saying. She asked again but no reply came. Then a rabbit leaped onto the hay stack and cuddled up to her, followed by a duck, a baby lamb and a large cart horse started to lick her hair.

"Oh, thank you that's very nice but I'm feeling hungry and I don't like the taste of this hay" that other animals were nibbling. Suddenly, she heard a voice in her head say.

"In that case you had better follow me to the farm house". She looked around trying to work out where the voice was coming from. When, she spotted a smiling face standing in the stable doorway.

"Hi. My name is Dungo and I own this farm and care for all the animals here. Follow me?"

She didn't feel nervous as she had never spoke nor seen anyone before her arrival in plant world. So, she stood up stroked the animals and said she would be back, and followed Dungo to the house. She had lots to eat and met Snowflake who lived in one of the buildings on the other side of the hill.

"Would you like to stay with me so that I can show you around" asked Snowflake.

"That would be lovely, but can I come each day to see the animals?" enquired Yuveliss.

"Of course, you can. I'm sure Dungo would be pleased of your help in looking after them. He may even show you how to heal those that are injured," replied Snowflake.

"Oh! That's fantastic I would love to heal them" said an excited Yuvelis.

Snowflake took her to The Old Oak Garden Centre and introduced her to all the Plant People, including Byron the librarian who had the knack of knowing which books a child would enjoy reading.

He took one look at her, read her mind, which Plant People can do and went off to find the books she would like. He came back with an armful that all had to do with things that make humans and animals healthier that he had found in the Human World that he often visited at night.

He would go there in search of the latest books that Plant People may enjoy reading. Of course, there were no books that contained any violence or that were sad stories.

Everything in Plant World was positive and uplifting, as being 'happy' was what Plant World was all about. For all plant people, as well as, all the animals, birds and insects that lived there in harmony with nature.

Although, she had recently arrived in Plant World she understood every written word and read and re-read every book before asking for others on healing.

Whoever she met she would ask them if they were feeling okay. If not, she would find out what was wrong with them and suggest a cure. She, like Dungo knew instantly what was wrong with an animal and helped it back to being well and full of energy.

She went to school with all the other plant children. But at playtime she would sit in a corner of the playground and the kids would come over to her, if they wanted some advice on how to keep fit and healthy. If anyone fell over and cut their knee, she was there in seconds cleaning it, and applying some natural substance before bandaging it.

When she left school, she decided to travel the world looking for injured plant people and animals. Widget the handyman designed a vehicle powered by sunlight that she took with her. It had beds in the back and a little operating table where she could mend broken limbs. Her greatest gift was the healing she gave through her hands that could mend and heal almost anything.

She went into the darkest of jungles searching for injured animals who knew when she was around as they all came looking for her. They included elephants with blocked trunks, lions with toothache, gorillas with strained muscles, ostriches with dirt in their eyes, crocodiles that couldn't stop crying.

A giraffe with a stiff neck where she had to ask the help of the monkeys who hung from a tree, one by one and held onto her while she massaged the poor animal.

She learnt to swim as she had to swim out to dolphins and whales that had sores on their backs.

She once had a huge python wrap itself around her while she found the cause of the stomach ache. It turned out to be a hedgehog it had eaten by mistake. She coaxed the hedgehog out as it was still alive and released it so it could join its friends. The python gave her a big kiss and unwound itself and slithered away.

She had to climb up the side of a mountain on one occasion as she learnt there was an eagle there with a broken wing. It was snowing and very cold getting there but when she arrived the eagle took her under his sound wing and warmed her. The Eagle had six baby eaglets that also wrapped themselves around her, and the male eagle brought her fish from a river that she shared with the eaglets and mother. She healed the wing and instead of having to climb down the mountain. The two eagles grasped her hands and floated her down back to her ambulance.

We will return one day to find out where she is and what animals she has been treating while we are away.

# VISITOR FIFTEEN= STEVEN THE PLANT EXPERT

Steven, a young boy, arrived in Plant World early one morning. Sitting in front of Widget's bicycle inside his storage shed. If you read the first series of The Secret World of the Plant People' you will know that Widget is the Plants Worlds' most famous handyman. He designed his bike that he used to transport things, including plant people who enjoyed travelling with him. It also had a crane to lift things.

Steven couldn't resist stroking all parts of the bike before sitting on it. He looked round to see other bikes and many gadgets and machines, such as grass cutters. In one corner was a stack of cycle spare parts which he wandered over to. He found a box full of tools which he started to use to create a bike. He even found cans of paint which he used to paint the bike with different colours.

Then, about midday, Widget came into the shed to find Steven sitting on his colorful bike,

"Hello young man. When did you create the bike, you are sitting on?" asked Widget. He often found new arrivals in plant world in his store room.

"This morning. Who are you?" replied Steven.

"I'm Widget the handyman and I've come to get my bike to take some timber and tools to build some tables for the Old Oak Garden Centre. Do you want to follow me on your bike?

"Oh! Yes please" smiled Steven. Before doing so he helped load Widgets bike. They then set off down the road. Where almost every plant person waved and cheered Widget as he passed them bye. A couple climbed on board also. Steven, thought that he must add a couple of seats to the next bike he built. They soon arrived at this huge garden canter, which is identical to mine in the human world.

Steven helped unload the timber and tools and while Widget started to build more tables. Steven started to wander around the garden canter. He loved what he saw. There were so many different varieties of flowers, plants, trees. He started to ask all the gardeners what each plant was called. They also told him what many plants were used for. Such as, eating, drinking, healing, and simply displaying, as they looked so beautiful, that made him smile and feel joyful.

He so enjoyed the first visit, that he returned each day to learn more about each plant and how to help them grow. On one occasion he wandered over to the Old Oak Tree as he sensed it had a message for him. Which it did. He placed his arms around the huge trunk.

"Hello Steven. I'm so pleased you have arrived in Plant world, as you are going to be a famous expert about caring for thousands of different plants." Explained TOOT, The Old Oak Tree.

"Wow, how am I going to be an expert?" enquired Steven.

"Carry on asking questions about what you see. Also, visit the professors of land management at Old Oak Academy. To learn how to design garden centers, and farms. I also, suggest you visit the Rainbow Room to learn how to heal damaged plants and trees." Suggested TOOT.

(I wrote about my experience of visiting the Rainbow Room in the 'The Secret World of Plant People' book. I've added the story after this chapter. As I hope, you the reader, will try and communicate with trees and plants, and heal them when needed.

Steven visited the university and told the professors what TOOT had told him. They were more than happy to teach him what they knew so far. Knowing, that one day Steven would be teaching them what he had discovered. Don't forget that there is no money in Plant World. Plant people just use their skills and talents to help anyone. The professors taught Steven how to grow different plants and how to keep them away from other plants and trees so they can expand as much as they want. They also, told him about the Plant World, just like the human world. Where each country had some different types of plants. Many, of which had still to be discovered.

They introduced Steven to Doc Pete Moss. Doc, is an expert at concocting new plant food formulas. He also, mixes different types of compost, to help the plants grow. He is also the hairiest plant person around. This is because, of all the plant enhancing ingredients, he is forever mixing with his hands.

He is also one of Plant world's, greatest explorers. He is forever visiting strange lands, in search of new natural products, that will both help plants, and plant people.

He has also been known, to pass on his findings, through thought waves, to biologists in the human world. They have then, gone on to discover medicines, that have helped, the human population. Doc suggested that Steven work with him and travel with him overseas. Which of course he happily did.

On one occasion they visited Miami where the famous singer Mudanna had a concert. Doc had met her before in England and invited her to the piece of land he was working on in Florida. Steven suggested that he would pick her up the following day and take her there. What she didn't realize was that he would turn up on a bicycle with another he had designed for her. It had a microphone sticking up from the handlebars and a pair of speakers hanging at the back. So, she could sing as she rode and passers-by would happily hear her.

They rode together along some narrow roads. Most of which were alongside rivers. Suddenly, an alligator leapt out of the river and stood in front of them with its mouth open. As you may know. In Plant World no one harms animals. Plus, many can communicate with them. Fortunately, Doc had taught Steven how to, as they met so many wild animals on their travels.

"Hello Ali. What a big mouth you have and lovely white teeth" said Steven using his mind.

"Yes. I have. You have a lovely lady riding with you" replied Ali who then closed his mouth and slid back into the river.

They eventually arrived at the land they were working on, and showed Mudanna what they had discovered. She was very impressed but apologized as she had to leave because she had another concert. So, Steven raced with her back to Florida.

Doc and Steve spent many weeks there. Steve set up surfing and water sport training programs. Before sailing over on Ted, the Crazy Cyclist's yacht to Sosua in the Dominican Republic. Ted lent Steven one of his racing bikes and showed him the land on the North coast He spotted many plants he had not seen before. Especially, on one piece of land in Sabaneta where he met the owner called Kirk. He had travelled the world and brought samples of plants which he was now growing but with difficulty. Steven took Doc to his land and together they studied each plant. They then asked Kirk if he would go to the Far East and collect more plants and bring them to the Dominican Republic.

Steven decided to stay there as there were so many varieties of medicinal plants which he started studying and experimenting with. Doc went back to the Old Oak Academy to teach students what he had learnt.

Doc also met Fernando, known as Wiki, in Sosua. Fernando spent most of his time studying the human world internet. That most plant people didn't because it is so depressing. However, Fernando helped some Plant people to pass on their experiences on social media sites that would help humans. He helped Steve promote the medicinal plants and the plants Kirk showed them by adding a website that human's thought was from another human expert.

As the years went by Steven gathered so much information about the Plants in Plant World, that he was invited to give lectures to students all over the world. He gave them all the following information.

# TREES HAVE CONSCIOUSNESS.

Seth kindly explained about Trees having consciousness, as well as, animals, having consciousness that you can read about later in appendix 3. I hope you will obtain a copy and read the whole book and do the exercises to help you to take control of your life. From 'The Unknown Reality', Volume 2 © 1979 by Jane Roberts, © 1996 by Robert F. Butts, © 2012 by Laurel Davies Butts Reprinted by permission of Amber-Allen Publishing, Inc., P.O. Box 6657, San Rafael, CA 94903. All rights reserved.

The proximity of so many trees has considerable health value, and to those doing psychic or other creative work the effects are particularly conducive to a peaceful state of mind. Trees are great users and yet conservators of energy, and they automatically provide much vitality to areas in which they are plentiful. This is physically obvious in scientific terms; the consciousness of trees is remarkably kind and enduring.

Now you think of dogs as friends of man, and you personify gods in human terms. You think of them sometimes as guardians. In those terms, now, trees are also guardians. They are attached to the people they know. You cannot put a leash on them and walk them around the block, yet trees form a protective barrier, about, say, a home or, neighbourhood. They are actually concerned. They have personalities-certainly to the same extent that dogs do, yet of an entirely different nature. They respond to you. The trees in that hill house neighbourhood then are particularly friendly, strong, and protective, and they will help renew your energies.

In your terms, language, presupposes a particular kind of development of mind, and when you think of language you tie the two together. There are languages that have nothing to do with words-or with thoughts as you understand them. Yet some of these communicate in a far more precise fashion.

Cellular transmission, for example, is indeed much more precise than any verbal language, communicating data so intricate that all of your languages together would fall far short of matching such complexity. This kind of communication carries information that a thousand alphabets could not translate. In such a way, one part of the body knows what is happening in every other part, and the body as a whole knows its precise position on the surface of the planet. It is biologically aware of all the other life-forms around it to the most minute denominator.

This applies to the future as well as the past. The body itself knows the source of water, for example, and food. Natives divorced from your technology do very well, as wild animals also do, in probing the life of the planet and their positions within it.

A simple tree deals with the nature of probabilities as it thrust forward into new seeds. Computations go on constantly within it, and that communication involves an inner kind of language innocent of symbols and vowels. The tree knows its present and future history, in your terms, but it understands a future that is not preordained. It feels its own power in the present as it constructs that future. In deeper terms the tree's seeds also realize that there is a future there- a variety of futures toward which they grope.

The following are additional notes added by Robert: Jane's husband- Seth's material on trees reminded me of his 18th session for January 22, 1964. It made a lasting impression upon me. It's full of evocative statements that were new to us at the time, since the sessions were barely underway: "As to Jane's feeling about trees having (a certain kind) of consciousness, of course this is the case. The tree is dissociated in one manner. It is in a state of drowsiness on the one hand, and on the other it focuses the usable portion of its energy into being a tree."

"The inner senses of the tree have a strong affinity with the properties of the earth itself. They feel their growing, as you listen to your heartbeat. They also experience pain (which) while definite, unpleasant, and sometimes agonizing, is not of an emotional nature in the same way that you might feel pain. It is if your breath were to be suddenly cut off."

"A tree knows human beings also... by the vibrations in the air as they pass, which hit the tree's trunk from varying distances, and even by such things as voices. The tree does not build up an image of man, but a composite sensation which represents an individual. And the same tree will recognize the same person who passes it by each day."

The consciousness of a tree is not as specifically focused as your own. Yet to all intents and purposes, the tree is conscious of 50 years before its existence, and 50 years hence. Its sense of identity spontaneously goes beyond the change of its own form. It has no ego to cut the "I" identification short.

Jane Roberts wrote this poem in 1964

The trees in the forest
Stand secret and silent,
Their voices suspended
In lungs of leaves,
That only can whisper
Of dreams held dormant,
That breathe only once
In a million years.
Deep is the sleep
Of the moss and the pebble.
Long is the trance
Of the grass and the meadow.
Footfalls come
And footfalls pass,
But no sound can break
That green-eyed trance.

# VISITOR SIXTEEN- THE RAINBOW ROOM

With Ms. Neatly in charge, Barker supervising everyone, and Widget building and repairing anything, and everything. My garden canter, began looking like it was, before the storm. it was almost ready, to receive the first customers. Except for, one vital missing ingredient. We had no healthy plants, flowers, bushes or trees to sell to the customers.

I knew, when we re-opened, that we would be swamped with customers. Because, they will be wanting to replace everything, they had lost in the storm. I couldn't see, how we could find, enough plants in time. All the growers, in Southern England, were in a similar situation.

All around me were damaged, bent and broken, plants and trees. It was a very sad sight for me. I always felt the pain, of plants in distress. Every morning, since I opened the Center. I would check, on each and every plant. I always greeted them, by their name. Some, I sensed, liked to be called by their English name, such as, Primrose or Bluebell. Whilst, the more mature and hardy plants, were more formal. They preferred to be called, by their Latin name.

When I was a small child, I had my own tiny garden. I grew wild flowers, that attracted butterflies and bees. I had long conversations with the plants. I told them about school, friends, and family. Whenever, I was feeling sad, their heads would move closer to me. If I mentioned, I had been hit by a school bully. They would visibly shake in anger.

As I grew older, I always carried, a water bottle around with me. I found, that so many shops and offices, neglected their plants. I could hear them begging for Water. But no one else seemed to hear their plea. I would water them. Then leave a card with the owner or member of staff, that said

'Dear Sir or Madam,

Will you please water me, and spray and trim my leaves?

Thank You,

Your affectionate plant.

I mentioned to Uncle Two Trees, my concerns about not having sufficient plants to sell. He assured me that everything would be ready on time. So, stop worrying.

"How, "I said. "Look at all those plants, lying on their sides, or hanging over the plant pots, bent and crushed".

"Why do you think we are called, 'Plant People'?" asked Uncle Twotrees.

"I never thought to ask. You don't look like plants. But you are different from humans, in color, size, and appearance".

"Come with me, to the canter, in plant world. I will show you, why" replied Uncle Twotrees.

I followed him to the corner of the garden, where a large building stood. I noticed, many plant people coming and going. All of them carrying plants.

I went inside. To my utter amazement, it was full of plant people. Each one, was standing in front of a plant, with their hands, gently caressing it.

The room was ablaze, with the colors of the rainbow. I had never seen such colors. in my whole life, before. I was overwhelmed, with the tremendous feeling of love, that filled every centimeter of the room. I just stood there in wonderment, trying to remember, to breathe.

Uncle Twotrees gently took my hand. He sat me in front of a small apple tree, lying in a large pot. Its trunk was nearly broken in two. The sight of it, bending over in pain, made my eyes, fill with tears. Uncle Twotrees lifted my hands and cupped them around, the broken trunk. He then simply said, "Give it your Love."

I sat there, with tears streaming down my cheeks. But I concentrated, all my loving energy. I then projected it towards the tree.

It looked like electricity, jumping and leaping, towards the tree. My hands were tingling and shaking with energy.

Then, to my amazement, and extreme pleasure, the tree began to straighten up. It was soon erect, and taller than it had ever been before. Plus, there was no sign of any damage.

I thought, there couldn't be, any better feeling, than what I was experiencing, at that moment. I was wrong.

Suddenly, from the top of the tree, came a brilliant white light. It curved towards me. Then came down, and touched my heart. I felt as though, my whole body, was lifted off the ground. An indescribable feeling. touched every fiber, and molecule in my body. It felt as though it lasted for hours. When in fact, it was only a few seconds.

Afterwards, Uncle Twotrees, explained what had happened.

"Every living thing, on your human planet, responds to love and attention, from something, or someone else. It could be a flower, thanking a bee, for taking its pollen, to another flower. Or a bird, removing ticks from the back of an animal. Or, a child being cared for, by its mother".

"You just experienced, a tree sending you its love and its energy. It was thanking you, for healing and restoring it to full health."

Very few humans realize. When you show an interest, or kindness, to a tree, plant, flower, or even a blade of grass. They sense that kindness. They respond, by sending you their form of love, in return".

"How often have you sat in a field. Looked around and thought, how beautiful everything looks. You may begin, to notice, swallows dancing in the wind, or the vivid color of buttercups and daises. Gradually, you begin to feel different. happier, lighter hearted."

"You put this down, to being outside in the fresh clear air, on a sunny day. When in fact. All the living things, around you, are thanking you, in their way, for appreciating their beauty. It is their love, that you are feeling, that lifts your spirit"

"If only humans realized. The more love you give, to living things. The more you will receive in return This is why, we are talking and showing ourselves to you today. You have always been kind, to plants, animals, and other human beings."

"We are so pleased to be able to return that kindness. Especially now, when you cannot see the way forward, from the devastation, caused by the hurricane. We have always been there, in the background, helping you. But now, we can show ourselves, and be part of your life, from now on".

I left the Rainbow room, a totally different person. To the one, that had entered. I had actually saved the life, of a tree, with my own hands, and thoughts of love. This was truly amazing. I knew, from that moment on, that everything was possible. I simply, could not believe, how happy I felt.

Read Appendix 1. About plants and trees having consciousness.

# VISITOR SEVENTEEN- CHARLES

A young adult who has spent many years reading the bible with the help of a tutor. Was sleeping and began dreaming. He suddenly appeared in Plant World where he met Seth, who he sensed he had met before.

"Hello Charles. It's been thousands of centuries since we first met" commented Seth.

"When was that" asked Charles.

"When I visited Earth as a Lumanian I taught other Lumanians how to care for everyone and not experience any harm or violence. They explored earth until homo sapiens began to appear who were violent. So, they began building cities below ground, so that we could stay clear of humans. I also introduced them to their god who focused on all Lumerians to make sure they survived the earthly life. He actually encouraged some of them to visit some peaceful humans, which you did Charles and married a lovely peaceful lady and had children. You taught the children and their friends not to have any violent moods and to help all living things, and become vegetarians." Explained Seth

"Oh! Yes, that's right. I remember many of our cities are still available under ground, especially in the Pyrenees mountains in Spain. Where I spent most of my time. But I recall passing away to another dimension." Commented Charles.

Seth explained that he returned to heaven where Jehovah taught him how to help energies in other dimensions, which is what I am always doing. We both returned to the earth. You were Adam and Eves second son, called Able. And I was their third son called Seth. Sadly, you left earth when your brother Cain killed you. You then returned in the 19th Century. Where you helped attract thousands of humans to learn about a god, the bible, and skills in living in the human world. You then returned to heaven but couldn't resist reincarnating and returned to earth. But you often revisited in your dream state, this dimension, called Plant World, where everyone cares for all living things. Which you enjoy exploring. Would you like to visit the heavenly dimension with me now, as there is an interesting lecture going on?

"Yes, please Seth"

Seth held his hand and took him through a number of dimensions very quickly before arriving in Heaven, where he heard lots of voices singing, just like the human witnesses he met in a weekly congress. He wandered over to an Amphitheatre were thousands of human looking energies were sitting and listening to a speaker on the stage. Charles couldn't believe who he saw, as it was Jesus. He sat down with Seth and listened to what Jesus was saying.

Jesus said that he was planning to return to the human world in 2075 to change all the religions. He wanted humans to care and protect all living things. Including fellow humans from other countries, animals and trees that he explained all had consciousness, just like all the atoms in the human bodies. I want to thank Seth for spending 30 years visiting the psychic medium Jane Roberts in the human world. He mentally took her over and explained about everything in the human world, and other dimensions, such as dream worlds, where they visit when the leave the human world. Jane's husband recorded every word and published them in ten books that became very popular in the 19th century. I'm hoping young adults read them this century so that they will help me change the world when I visit again. I also hope that Charles will encourage the organization he visits ever week, that has millions of members all over the world who help everyone else. I'm sure they will help me in 2075. I also hope that many of you listening to me will arrange to return to earth where you can select your parents and the skills you will have to support me when I arrive.

Everyone in the Amphitheatre started cheering and singing "Yes, Yes, Yes, we will all be there to meet you.

Charles returned to earth remembering this amazing dream and began trying to encourage more humans to read the bible and Seth books. So, they understood how they could help change the world by accessing their inner consciousness.

# VISITOR EIGHTEEN- WOODY CLEVE THE CARPENTER

A dream boy arrived in Plant World, sitting on a Dominican Republic cliff surrounded by trees. Below him on the beach were branches, tree trunks that had fallen down from the cliff, or floated onto the beach. For some reason he began climbing down the cliff. On route he met a number of seagulls of which most were asleep, so he passed them quietly. Some he chatted to. They told him where he was. He reached the beach and looked around and found a rusty machete. He picked it up and for some reason he swiped one of the dead tree branches and cut it in half. He then went along swinging and chopping other dead trees lying on the beach.

He gathered all the pieces he chopped and placed them on a large rock partly on the beach and in the ocean. He started to clean the machete and began sharpening it by rubbing it against the silicon rock. He then used it to smooth and shape different lengths of timber.

As he sat on the rock. He noticed someone standing on a windsurf board. Then leaping in the air. He was so impressed that he started clapping and cheering him. It was the famous Surfer who had a surfing school further along the beach. He spotted the child and went over and suggested he climb aboard. He noticed all the pieces of wood that he had cut and shaped. Some of which the child was carrying along with his machete. He carefully, sailed him to his surf centre where he showed him the surf boards that he used to teach plant people.

Uncle Twotrees happened to be there and started talking to the child that explained what he had been cutting and shaping after climbing down the cliff.

"I can see that you are going to be a very skilled carpenter. I am therefore going to name you 'Woody Cleve', as Cleve means Cliffs in the human world. Announced Uncle Twotrees.

Cozette the interior designer was also on the beach learning how to surf. She suggested to Woody that he comes to her Dominican apartment and workshop. Where she will feed and look after him. He happily went with her after telling Surfer that he is going to start making surf boards for him.

Cozette had a three-bedroom apartment above a workshop where she had skilled plant people who made furniture that she designed. There was also a lovely showroom where visitors could choose what they wanted for free.

Woody spent every day in the workshop learning how to use all the tools and equipment to build and repair things. He went to the garden outside and found stacks of timber. While there a three- wheeler driven by Gracious Peat arrived stacked full of bits of timber.

"Where did you get these" asked Woody Cleve.

"Hi. I'm a grass cutter and gardener. When I find any dead tree or timber lying on the ground, that I think Cozette may use to make something. I bring it to her.' Explained Gracious Peat.

He then pointed to a stack of timber in the corner that looked different from the timber he brought. "Those were spotted by Jessie Agnes the sailor while cruising along the coast. She arranged with her friends Ted and Alan the cyclists to go with me to help lift them."

As Woody grew older. He began creating some beautiful pieces of furniture, as well as, art work that plant people hung on their walls. He also, of course, built some extremely smooth and fast kite boards. One of which he used to travel along the coast looking for pieces of timber on the beach.

The Dean of Old Oak Academy heard about Cleves carpentry skills and invited him to become a tutor. Which Cleve happily agreed to do. He taught many age groups, not only about carpentry, but also a number of other subjects that his students enjoyed. Dean realized he was a natural educator. So, he asked him if he would start teaching dream teenagers that just entered Plant World. How to care for everyone. This he happily did. He taught them so many ways of helping fellow plant people, such as, building houses and gardens. Designing furniture and interior rooms that he found teenage girls were more creative in doing. He also taught the boys how to build places for animals, such as, kennels, and stables. In the same lesson he would encourage them to help save animals, and insects, such as bees, that were drowning. He soon learnt that trees had consciousness so he never actually cut branches of a live tree. Each morning on route to the academy, he stopped and chatted to TOOT 'The Old Oak Tree'. (You can read about TOOT in my book 'The Secret World of Dream Animals and Plants'.)

# VISITOR NINETEEN-HUMPHREY THE OSTRICH

When an Ostrich saves the life of a human its wing feathers grow and it can fly to heaven where they become angels. They often return in many disguises to help humans. But they don't know this until it happens, as Humphrey below is about to find out. When he next returned to the human world, he goes looking for his Ostrich brother and sister. To tell them what happened to him and to warn them.

He finds them in the desert with their heads stuck in the sand. There are many Ostriches but he can recognize his family just by looking at their rear. He creeps up to them and nibbles their behinds. They all jump in the air, not knowing what bit them.

They swivel their heads to see Humphrey standing there smiling. They were so pleased to see him. They came over and gave him a kiss and a cuddle. Humphrey was embarrassed and asked them to follow him to a quiet spot. Away from the others who still had their heads in the sand.

"I came to tell you all about Ostrich heaven where I have been for the past year."

"Here he goes again. Telling us unbelievable stories" said his sister Clarissa.

"Now, wait a minute. I may have exaggerated the truth a little when I lived here," replied Humphrey who felt like sticking his head in the sand at this moment,

"A little" said his big brother Winston. "What about the time you told us you had fought off, single handed. Polar bears that were floating on an iceberg who tried to land in Australia."

"I did too, I didn't want them to stay in Australia. As they were huge and would have attacked us all. I frightened them off and they jumped back on the iceberg"

"That was in the middle of summer I recall" said a disbelieving Tabitha his youngest sister.

"Okay, tell us more about Ostrich heaven" said Winston.

"It was night time and I heard the water buffalos bellowing. So, I went to investigate. I found them surrounding this human about to charge him. So, I crept up behind the biggest buffalo and pecked his personal bits. He just up and ran as did all the other buffalos. The human came up to me. He stroked my head, and thanked me for saving his life.

All of a sudden, my wings began to grow and grow. Before I knew it. I was flying high above the ground with the human waving me good bye. I just kept going upwards towards the silver moon. When I suddenly found myself on a cloud and as I sank into it. This beautiful countryside appeared with rivers, waterfalls, soft sandy mounds. Then to my amazement two ostriches appeared and stood by my side. It was my mum and dad. But how could it be? They were run over a year ago, but it was them. They told me I was in Ostrich heaven. They said I could go back to Australia, any time I wanted, because I had saved a human life. It was so peaceful there, with no cars, no one chasing us, that I decided to stay?"

"If that's true, what are you doing here?" asked Tabitha.

"In heaven you can see into the future. I saw these aborigine children in danger. I thought I must help them. In an instant, I found myself back here."

"Where are they now" asked a disbelieving Winston.

"They are at the other end of the valley. I need your help to chase them out of the valley."

"Why should we do that" asked Tabitha.

"If you look behind you in the distance, you will see why." Answered Humphrey.

They all turned their heads and to their surprise. They saw smoke rising above the hills.

"Oh, No. Forest fire. Quickly tell everyone to head for the river at the end of the valley." Instructed Winston.

Suddenly, three ostriches became 30 then 300.They all spread out to tell all the other animals in the valley to run for it. Many of the ostriches picked up the slower animals and plonked them on their backs. Humphrey and Tabitha went ahead to warn the aborigine children, who were camped further along the valley. Some kangaroos joined them. Together they kicked, punched and pecked the children until they ran towards the river. Had they stayed. They would have been trampled to death. By all the animals that were escaping the flames, that were roaring down the windy valley.

The aborigine children crossed the river and told their parents about being pecked and kicked. The elder of the tribe looked across the river and saw the animals trying to cross and escape the ever-closing flames. He immediately knew the Ostrich and Kangaroos had saved the lives of their children. So, he ordered the whole village to help as many animals as they could. To cross the river and up the steep banks.

Some aborigines crossed over in boats. They helped the animals that were afraid of the water, to get across the river to safety.

Thousands of birds and animals were saved that day because of Humphrey warning them, in time to escape. Winston and Tabitha never again doubted the stories told by Humphrey.

# VISITOR TWENTY- BERTIE THE BEAR

"I wonder where I'm off to this month" thought Bertie. I do hope it's to a happy home with lots of toys to play with. It's always a worrying moment sitting here in school watching all the children passing me by. I wonder which one will stop, pick me up and take me home. I can usually tell from the first touch what they will be like. Some of the boys are a little rough. They just grab me and throw me in their school satchel. Amongst the books and pens which can be very uncomfortable. I like to see where I am going and watching the humans passing me by. Some of them even recognize me and call out "Hello Bertie, How's your new home?" I just smile back.

"Oh! Oh! who's this coming towards me. It's a little girl who I have seen in school many times. Let's see if I can remember her name. Aargh! Yes, I remember its Emily? She should be fun, as she is always talking and doing things. Here we go she's picking me up and giving me a big cuddle. Now I just have to wait until the afternoon and go home with her. I wonder what type of house she lives in. I hope it has a garden.

What's going on? The teacher is picking me up. Where is she taking me? Maybe she's going to hand me over to Emily's father, as he drops her here, most mornings. There he is. He looks a little surprised. I hope he likes me? He's now taking me to the car and placing me in the passenger seat. I hope he remembers to fasten my seat belt. I seem to remember Emily saying he is a fast driver. He looks a nice chap and hopefully he will take me for rides in his car."

The father takes Emily and Bertie home where he spots Emily's mother. She too often took Emily to school in a buggy. She actually takes them both in the buggy to a local park. Where Emily plays with Bertie. She takes him up the steps to a slide and together they slide down. They then go over to the swings and she places Bertie on one of them that has a frame. She sits on another swing. Their mother then pushes them both. Much to Bertie's surprise.

Emily then placed Bertie in a haversack with his head sticking out. She placed it on her back and began climbing quite a tall climbing frame. Bertie was a little nervous at first. But he enjoyed the view from the top of the frame. Especially, the tall trees that he began to talk to with his mind.

They then went back home. Where the mother gave them some food. As he sat at the table, he felt something brush his feet. He looked down and spotted a pussy cat. He gave it some of the food he had. Then later while sleeping on the bed with Emily. The cat joined them and started licking him. He stroked it. Then began talking to her, unbeknown to Emily. The cat told him her name was Katie and that she was a healer. She knew when any of the family had a health problem. She would then climb on the person and start massaging the spot.

You may be surprised to learn that a number of dogs and cats have healing abilities. Also, some house plants are also aware when someone in the house is unwell, or even pregnant and about to have a baby.

# VISITOR TWENTY-ONE- GIANTS CAUSEWAY

Uncle Twotrees told me about Plant people who centuries ago. Visited Earth and began building underground cities in order to monitor what humans were doing. They called themselves Lumanians. He told me recently that some children that entered a tunnel underground. This is what happened.

It was Christmas Day and a family had just opened all their presents and were happy reading and playing with their gifts. Daddy said "Let's go for a walk after lunch, but where shall we go to?"

"Let's go to The Giants Causeway", replied Anna.

"Good idea' said mummy "The sea air will wake us all up, but we must wrap up as it will be very cold and windy there.'

They all had a lovely Christmas Lunch and thanked mummy for all the work she had to do to make it so tasty. They then went to their rooms and got dressed in their warm jackets with hoods, and gloves. Then headed for the car. But not before Anna picked up a penny whistle, she had been given for Christmas.

"Why are you taking that?" asked Jemima.

"I don't know but I had this voice in my head telling me to take it" replied Anna.

"How odd but please don't practice in the car" asked Jemima.

They soon arrived at the Giant's Causeway as it was very quiet on the roads and Daddy pretends, he is a racing driver when he gets behind the wheel.

Mummy held Anna's hand, and Daddy held Jemima's hand as it was quite slippery. The waves were crashing onto the stones in the sea. They wandered around the area and even climbed to the top of a pile of stones. Anna, pointed to a pathway and suggested they head in that direction, which they did after carefully climbing down the pile of stones. As they walked down a corridor of tall stones, Anna suddenly went over and touched one and said "Okay."

She then proceeded to play her penny whistle for the first time. Strange sounding notes floated in the air, when suddenly to their amazement, a door appeared in the stone wall in front of them. Anna walked towards it still playing her penny whistle. The door opened and just before she stepped inside, Mummy grabbed hold of her hand and went inside with her. Daddy and Jemima tried to follow them but the door suddenly disappeared. Daddy tried kicking and thumping the stone but the door didn't appear.

Jemima said we must call the police or fire brigade. Daddy, got his mobile out and dialled 999 and told the person on the other end what had just happened.

"Excuse me sir, but have you been celebrating Christmas with too much wine" asked the operator.

"No, I haven't" and handed the phone to Jemima who confirmed what had just happened.

"Oh! Okay I'll send a police car straight away" replied the operator.

Meanwhile, Mummy and Anna hugged each other as it was pitch black and they were afraid to move an inch forward in case there was a hole in front of them.

"Could we please have some light" called out Anna.

To their amazement the whole place lit up and there before them was some steps leading downwards. Mummy wasn't sure what to do as she too had tried opening the door in the dark that had disappeared behind her. She looked again at where the door had been and to her amazement. She could see Daddy and Jemima as though she was looking through a window. She started to bang on the window but it felt like stone. She started to shout but she could tell they could not hear her, but she could hear them talking on the mobile phone and was pleased that the police were on their way.

Anna pulled Mummy's hand and said "We should go down those steps" and started to walk in that direction. As they stepped onto the first step, the steps suddenly began slowly moving like an escalator. They just stood there as they descended and looked at the walls on either side that where full of drawings and colorful paintings.

"What are those animals" asked Anna.

"They look like prehistoric animals" replied Mummy.

"Oh yes. I can see a huge mammoth and a saber-toothed tiger" said Anna.

Then near the bottom of the staircase they looked up and nearly fell down as there on the ceiling was a huge lifelike drawing of a Tyrannosaurus with its mouth open as if it was going to jump down and eat them.

"Don't worry it's only a painting" said Mummy who kept looking upwards to make sure she was correct.

They arrived at the bottom that looked like an underground platform as there appeared to be a railway line with no track but dark holes at either end.

A voice suddenly said "Stand back please your train is about to arrive."

Mummy grabbed hold of Anna and leant back against the wall. She then heard a sort of whistling sound followed by a bright light that appeared from one end of the tunnel. Within seconds a sort of

train made of colored glass appeared and stopped in front of them and a door of blue light opened. They nervously stepped inside but as they did so a soft sounding voice said

"Welcome Mummy and Anna to the world of Lumania. The train of light will take you to our leader who will return you to Daddy and Jemima later today."

Mummy looked amazed at Anna who was smiling and began dancing. The train began to move but they felt no sensation, even as they looked out the window and saw they were travelling at an incredible speed. Within what felt like only a few minutes the train came to a halt and many doors opened and in stepped these human looking individuals. They were thin looking and wearing brilliant white clothes that reminded Mummy of ancient Greeks. They all had a sort of glow of different colors around them known as auras.

They spotted Mummy and Anna and suddenly rushed to another compartment where they stood behind a closed door and looked at them. Anna smiled and waved at them, then started to play her penny whistle. As she did so she noticed that they too began to smile and slowly some began to move back into the carriage. One of them came over and introduced himself as Casiel.

"Could you tell me who you are and where we are going" asked a somewhat nervous Mummy.

"With pleasure! We are Lumanians who you may not have heard about but we have been living underground for centuries. Our ancestors were from Atlantis that sank before you humans arrived on this lovely planet of Earth.

"Why do you live underground?" asked Anna who went over and touched Cashel's hand.

"Good question. We did live above ground for a while but then you humans started to appear. You were very violent and this scared us. So, we created cities underground using advanced technologies created in Atlantis that you humans have not yet invented.

The train suddenly stopped and more Lumanians climbed on board.

"Do we get off here" asked Anna?

"No. This is Paris as you can see on the map of the underground train above your head" said Casiel.

They both looked at the map which showed stations all over Europe and different routes that all ended in Egypt. The train carried on at fantastic speed, smoothly stopping at stations that Casiel told them where they were.

"Are we going to Egypt" asked Mummy nervously?

"Yes, that is where most of us live and where our leaders have their headquarters" replied Casiel.

"What does everyone do when they get off the train" asked Anna?

"They are visiting ancient sites, where the 'Watchers' used to live observing what the humans were up to."

"Are you saying that you are tourists" enquired Mummy looking very surprised?

"Yes, many centuries ago our ancestors left Earth and moved to other worlds, such as Plant World, to see what was going on. We come back sometimes just to see what's happening and to see what our ancestors built and how they lived" answered Casiel.

"Are those stones in the Giant's Causeway from the tunnels they made" asked Anna.

"Yes Anna, you are very clever to have realized that" replied Casiel.

"How on Earth did they cut them and move them there" asked Mummy.

"They used sound which they taught to some humans, such as, Egyptian architects who built the pyramids" explained Casiel.

"Oh! so they met with humans" asked Mummy.

"That's correct. They tried to change the Neanderthals violent behaviour by marrying some of them whose children became what you call homo-sapiens. Sadly, many children still enjoyed fighting so they returned to the cities underground where they mentally kept in touch with those children who grew up to love all living things," answered Casiel.

"Do these humans still live on Earth" asked Mummy?

"Of course, you and Anna are two of them, as are all your ancestors, including your granny who keeps in regular touch with us" said Casiel.

"Was it you who told me to take my penny whistle to the Giant's Causeway" asked Anna?

"Not me personally but all Lumanians/humans have Lumanian guides who watch their every move and send suggestions to their brain when they are unsure what to do" explained Casiel.

"Was it my guide who suggested I buy the penny whistle for Anna "asked Mummy?

"I would think so, as the guides have the gift of being able to see into the future and knew that you were both going to visit us underground" said a thoughtful Casiel.

The train came to a halt. Casiel took both their hands and lead them along the platform to a staircase that moved downwards. Until suddenly before them was a city full of buildings as far as the eye could see. It was brightly lit and they stood there watching the Lumerians going about their business. They spotted a group of children going into what looked like a school, where they began playing ball games and having fun.

"Can we go and talk to those children over there" asked Anna.

"Why not, let's go now before they go into their classrooms" suggested Casiel.

He took them down on an elevator. Then to their surprise they found themselves on a pavement that was moving. So, they didn't have to walk. They simply glided over to the school, passing other Lumerians along the way who were also gliding but in different directions. They entered the school playground and immediately all the children came rushing to meet them as they had never seen humans before. They each introduced themselves and asked lots of questions. Before handing Anna, a ball and started playing 'tag' that Anna loved playing. The teachers came out and started to talk with mummy.

" Would you like to come to assembly and tell the children what it is like to live in the Human world" asked the headmistress.

"Yes, I would love to" replied Mummy.

They all went into a large assembly hall where Mummy began to talk to them. Anna sat in the front row giggling as Mummy described her childhood. She was then asked to go on stage and answer questions from the children, which she did. Everyone, started to cheer and applaud her and asked her to come back and talk to them again. She said she wasn't sure if she could find her way back but would ask her friend Casiel. As she would love to join their classes and learn all about them and Lumeria.

"We have to go and see our leader now" whispered Casiel to Mummy.

Mummy took hold of Anna's hand and they both waved goodbyes.

"Hope to see you soon" said Anna and wandered off the stage and followed Casiel to a huge golden colored building. Where all the colors of the rainbow shined from hundreds of windows. They entered a room where sat an ancient looking man who invited them to sit beside him.

"Hello, my name is Seth I'm so pleased to meet you at last Mummy. I have been watching you since you were a small child, as you travelled with your mother to many countries. Such as, Hong Kong where we arranged for you to meet with daddy. You may not realize this but Anna here chose you and daddy as her parents. As she knew you would give her all the love and attention, she would need on this visit to Earth"

"Pardon! I don't understand" said Mummy

"You humans don't realize that you keep returning to Earth to experience things. You choose your moment of birth, your location, your name, your parents, and your physical and mental condition. Many children remember their previous life but soon forget as they get older and often forget why they came to Earth this time. We Lumanians are here to help you to remember, but so many of you ignore our messages and intuitions. That is why you are here today to remind you, especially Anna. She has an important role to play on this visit to Earth. Everyone, who meets her falls in love with her and wants to help her in any way they can. They feel so happy and proud in doing so. That they start to look for other people, they can help and support. You will be surprised how many millions of people begin to feel the same way. Also, how the world will become a happier and healthier place to live. As they also begin to care for Mother Nature.

"What about my sister Jemima" asked Anna,

"Before you came to Earth you asked if she would join you and help you on this visit. She is a very intelligent girl who will use her many skills to assist you and others in this world. Your mummy is going to be very proud of you both. I suggest that when you return to Lumania you bring her along to the school. As there are secrets, she will learn that will help to teach people on Earth" suggested Seth.

"I think it's about time you returned to the Giants Causeway as Daddy and Jemima are getting really worried and the fire brigade is about to arrive.'

"They took their time as I heard Johnny talking to someone about what had happened" said Mummy.

"Augh! I forgot to mention that time in Lumania is totally different. What seems like many hours is in fact only a few minutes in the human world. When you go back, I suggest you don't mention what you have seen. That is, until you bring Jemima back to the same spot where Casiel will meet you and bring you here" advised Seth.

They all hugged each other before being taken back to The Giants Causeway where Casiel took them to a small cave just a few yards from where they had entered the magical doorway. They stepped outside after kissing and thanking Casiel for all his help. They found themselves in a corridor of rocks. Ahead of them where police and firemen trying to make a hole in the stone where they had entered Lumania. They casually walked over to them and tapped Daddy on the shoulder.

"What's going on" asked Mummy.

Daddy turned round and couldn't believe his eyes.

"Where did you come from" asked a surprised but very relieved father.

"We came out of the cave over there that we went into" replied Mummy crossing her fingers.

"What, but you went through this stone wall here, ask Jemima" said Johnny who hadn't noticed that Anna had been talking to Jemima.

"I told you we were looking at the wrong spot" answered Jemima,

Upon hearing this, the police and firemen started to move away. Muttering about another instance of someone who had celebrated too much on Christmas day.

After they had gone, Mummy took Daddies arm and said

"Thank you so much for trying to find us. Let's go home and have a rest. I feel exhausted."

This they did. Mummy drove them home as Johnny kept shaking his head and looked bewildered. That evening Anna told Jemima what had happened, and that they will be going back there with her. But she mustn't tell anyone. Her father started to read the following Seth book that explained all about Lumanians that you may find surprising.

# LUMANIANS



The Lumanians were a very thin, weakly people, physically speaking, but psychically either brilliant or completely ungifted. In some, you see, the built-in controls caused so many blockages of energy in all directions that even their naturally high telepathic abilities suffered.

They formed energy fields around their own civilization. They were, therefore, isolated from contact with other groups. They did not allow technology to destroy them, however. More and more of them realized that the experiment was not a success. Some, after physical death, left to join those from the previous successful civilization who had migrated to other planetary systems within the physical structure.

Large groups, however, simply left their cities, destroyed the force fields that had enclosed them and joined the many groups of relatively uncivilized peoples, mating with them and bearing children. These Lumanians died quickly, for they could not bear violence nor react to it violently. They felt however, that their mutant children might have a resulting disinclination toward violence, but without the prohibiting nerve-control reactions, with which they were endowed.

Physically the civilization simply died out. Some few of the mutant children formed a small later group who travelled the area as itinerants in the following century, with large bands of animals. They cared for each other mutually and many of the old legends concerning half-man and half-beast have come down through the ages simply from the memory of these old associations.

These people, as remnants, really, of the first great civilization, always carried within themselves strong subconscious memories of their origin. I am speaking of the Lumanians now. This accounted for their quick rise, technologically speaking. But because their purpose was so single-minded — the avoidance of violence- rather, say, than the constructive peaceful development of creative potential. Their experience was highly one-sided. They were driven by such a fear of violence. That they dared not allow the physical system freedom even to express it.

The vitality of the civilization was therefore weak — not because violence did not exist, but because freedom of energy and expression was automatically blocked along specific lines, and from outside physically. They well understood the evils of violence in earthly terms but they would have denied the individual's right to learn this his own way and thus prevented the individual from using his own methods, creatively, to turn the violence into constructive areas. Free will in this respect was discarded.

As a child is physically protected from some diseases for a while after he emerges from his mother's womb- so for a brief period is the child cushioned against some psychic disasters for a short period after birth, and carries within him, still for his comfort for memories of past existences and places. So, the Lumanians, for generations were supported by deep subconscious memories of the civilization that had gone before. Finally, however, these began to weaken. They had protected themselves against violence but not against fear.

They were, therefore, subject to all of the ordinary human fears which were then exaggerated, since, physically they could not respond even to nature with violence if attacked, they had to flee. The fight-or-flight principle did not apply. They had but one recourse.

Their god symbol was a male one — a strong, physically powerful male figure who would therefore protect them since they could not protect themselves. He evolved through the ages as their beliefs did, and into him they projected those qualities that they could not themselves express.

He was much later to appear as the old Jehovah, the God of Wrath who protected the Chosen People. The fear of natural forces was, therefore, initially extremely strong in them for the reasons given and brought about a feeling of separation between man and those natural forces that nurtured him. They could not trust the earth since they were not allowed to protect themselves against violent forces within it.

Their vast technology and their great civilization were largely underground. They were, in those terms, the original cavemen and they came out from their cities through caves also. Caves were not just places of protection in which unskilled natives squatted. They were often doorways to and from the cities of the Lumanians. Long after the cities were deserted, the following natives, uncivilized, found these caves and the openings.

In the period that you now think of as the Stone Age, the men you think of as your ancestors, the cavemen often found shelter not in rough naturally formed caves, but in mechanically created channels that reached behind them, and in the deserted cities in which once the Lumanians dwelled. Some of the tools fashioned by the cavemen were distorted versions of those they had found.

While the civilization of the Lumanians was highly concentrated, in that they made no attempt to conquer others or to spread out to any great extent in an area, they did set out, over the centuries, outposts from which they could emerge and keep track of the other native peoples.

These outposts were constructed underground. From the original cities and large settlements there were, of course, underground connections, a system of tunnels, highly intricate and beautifully engineered. Since these were an aesthetic people, the walls were lined with paintings and drawings, and sculpture was also displayed along these inner byways.

There were various escalated systems, some conveying people on foot, some conveying goods. It was not practical to construct such tunnels to the many outposts, however, which were fairly small communities and relatively self-supporting; some were a good distance away from the main areas of commerce and activity.

These outposts were situated in many scattered areas, but there were a fairly large number of them in what is now Spain and the Pyrenees. There were several reasons for this, one having to do with the existence of rather giant-sized men in the mountain areas. Because of the timid nature of these (Lumanian) people they did not enjoy outpost existence, and only the bravest and most confident of them were given such an assignment, which was temporary to begin with.

The following is a comment by Jane Roberts husband. It's interesting to note however that in late July, 1971, about eight months after this session, newspapers carried the story — with photographs — of the unearthing of a "massive" subhuman skull in a cave in the French Pyrenees Mountains, very close to the Spanish border. (The skull is at least two hundred thousand years old, and represents a race not identified before. It is now tentatively thought that several primitive races existed in Europe at that time. The period predates Neanderthal Man, and marks the start of the next-to-last Ice Age. This region in southern France is noted for its many caverns, easily eroded out of the limestone bedrock by flowing water. Jane has no paleontological background.)

The caves, again, served as doorways opening outward and often what seemed to be the back of a cave was instead constructed of a material opaque from the outside but transparent from the inside. The natives of the area using such caves for natural shelter, could therefore be observed without danger. These people reacted to sounds that are not audible to your ears. Their peculiar fear of violence intensified all of their mechanisms to an amazing degree. They were forever alert and on guard.

This is difficult to explain but they could mentally pitch a thought along certain frequencies- a highly distinguished art- and then translate the thought at a given destination in any of a number of ways into form or color, for example, or even into a certain type of image. Their language was extremely discriminating in ways that you could not understand, simply because gradations in pitch, frequency, and spacing were so precise and complicated.

Communication, in fact, was one of their strongest points and it was developed to such a high degree simply because they feared violence so deeply and were constantly on the alert. They banded together in large family groups, again in need for protection. Contact between children and parents was at a very high level and children were acutely uncomfortable if out of the sight of their parents for any amount of time.

For these reasons, those individuals who ran the outposts felt themselves to be in a very uncomfortable situation. They were limited in numbers and largely cut off from the main areas of their own civilization. They developed, therefore, an even greater telepathic activity, and a rapport with the earth above their head, so that the slightest tremor or footstep and the most minute movements above that were not usual, were instantly noted.

There were frequent peepholes, so to speak, through to the surface, from which they could make observations, and cameras situated there that kept the most precise pictures not only of the earth, but of the stars. Of course, they had complete records of underground gas areas and intimate knowledge of the inner crusts, keeping careful watch upon and anticipating earth tremors and faults. They were as triumphant about their descent into the earth as any race ever was who left the earth.

This was, as I told you, the second, and perhaps most interesting of the three civilizations. The first followed generally your own line of development and faced many of the problems that you now do. They were largely situated in what you call Asia Minor, but they were also expansive and travelled outward to other areas. These are the people I mentioned earlier who finally went on to other planets within other galaxies, and from whom the people of the Lumanian civilization came.

Now: Before we discuss the third civilization, there are a few more points I would like to make about the second one.

This has to do with communication as it was applied to their drawings and paintings, and to the highly discriminating channels that their creative communications could take. In many ways their art was highly superior to your own, and not as isolated. The various art forms, for example, were connected in a fashion that is nearly unknown to you, and because you are so unfamiliar with the concept, it will be rather difficult to explain.

Consider, for example, something very simple — say a drawing of an animal. You would perceive it simply as a visual object, but these people were great synthesizers. A line was not simply a visual line, but according to an almost infinite variety of distinctions and divisions, it would also represent certain sounds that would be automatically translated.

An observer could automatically translate the sounds before he bothered with the visual image, if he wanted to. In what would appear to be a drawing of an animal, then, the entire history or background of the animal might also be given. Curves, angles, lines all represented, beside their obvious objective function in a drawing, a highly complicated series of variations in pitch, tone and value; or if you prefer, invisible words.

Distances between lines were translated as sound pauses, and sometimes also as distances in time. Colour was used in terms of language in communication, in drawings and paintings; representing somewhat as your own colour does, emotional gradations. The colour however, its value of intensity, served to further refine and define- for example, either by reinforcing the message already given by the objective value of the lines, angles, and curves, and by the invisible word messages already explained; or by modifying these in any given number of ways.

The size of such drawings also spoke its own message. In one way this was a highly stylized art, and yet, it allowed for both great preciseness of expression in terms of detail, and great freedom in terms of scope. It was obviously highly compressed. This technique was later discovered by the third civilization, and some of the remnants of drawings done in imitation of it still exist. But the keys to interpretation have been completely lost, so, all you could see would be a drawing devoid of the multisensual elements that gave it such great variety. It exists, but you could not bring it alive.

I should perhaps mention here that some of the caves, particularly in certain areas of Spain and the Pyrenees, and some earlier ones in Africa, were artificial constructions. Now these people moved mass with sound and as I told you earlier, actually conveyed matter through a high mastery of sound. This is how their tunnels were originally formed, and it was also the method used to form some of the caves in areas where originally there were few. Often drawings on the cave walls were highly stylized information, almost like signs in your terms in front of public buildings, portraying the type of animals and beings in a given area.

These drawings later were used as models by your early cavemen in the historical times, to which you usually refer.

Now: Their communicative abilities, and therefore creative abilities, were more vital, alive, and responsive than yours are. When you hear a word, you may be aware of a corresponding image in your mind. With these people, however, sounds automatically and instantly built up an amazingly vivid image, that was not three-dimensional by any means, being internalized, but was far more vivid than your usual mental images indeed.

Certain sounds, again, were utilized to indicate amazing distinctions in terms of size, shape, direction, and duration, both in space and time. Sounds automatically produced brilliant images, in other words. For this reason, there was an easy distinction between what was called inner sight and outer sight, and it was quite natural for them to close their eyes when seated in conversation in order to communicate more clearly, enjoying the ever-changing and immediate inner images that accompanied any verbal interchange.

They learned quickly, and education was an exciting process, because this multisensuous facility automatically impressed information upon them not simply through one sense channel at a time but utilizing many simultaneously. For all this, however, and the immediacy of their perceptions, there was an inherent weakness. The inability to face up to violence and learn to conquer it meant, of course, that they also severely hampered a certain thrusting-out characteristic. Energy was blocked in these areas so that they actually lacked a forceful quality or sense of power.

I do not necessarily mean physical power however, but so much of their energy was used to avoid any meeting with violence that they were not able to channel ordinary aggressive feelings, for example, into other areas.

# VISITOR TWENTY-TWO – CAT THE MAGIC YELLOW DIGGER

Anna, loved the countryside. Especially the horses that she fed in the fields close by. Mummy and Daddy often took her and Jemima for walks and car rides. Anna was very good at seeing things before anyone else. That's why she enjoyed going to the big city as there was so much to see there.

On Christmas Day Anna was secretly given a yellow and black digger by Father Christmas. She had so much fun playing with it, that she took it with her everywhere she went. It was called Cat, as it moved around so quickly and could climb hills because of its big rear wheels.

After Christmas, Daddy said "Who wants to go and see the lights in the big city?"

"Me' replied Anna immediately. So, the following day they loaded up the car strapped everyone in and placed Cat beside Anna.

"It looks as though it may snow," said Mummy.

"Not to worry we will be back before it starts to lie on the ground", replied Daddy.

So off they went and as they neared the city the snow began to fall. Anna noticed so many things she hadn't seen before. She told everyone in the car what she spotted. Their heads started to spin looking from one side to the other. They went to a big store that had lots of signs saying 'For Sale'. But there where so many people that they could hardly move. Anna' said to herself, "I wish we had more room to see things?"

Then, all of a sudden, a very loud horn was heard that came from Cat, that she was holding. It was so loud that people were jumping out of the way to avoid the noise. Some went running out of the big shop. So, there was now room to move and see things. Anna looked down at Cat who had stopped making the noise. She thought she saw its headlight 'blink'. Anna thought no more of it and enjoyed looking at the toys and clothes. Mummy bought Anna and Jemima woolly hats that covered their ears and warm gloves, as it was getting colder. Daddy bought Mummy a really long woolen scarf and gave her a kiss while he wound it round and round her neck.

"Do I get a kiss for wearing my hat" asked Anna.

"Of course, you do" and both of them kissed her on each cheek.

"What about Jemima?"

"Oh, we can't forget about Jemima. So, Mummy picked her up. While Daddy picked up Anna. Each had a big hug and kisses all-round the shops before going back to the car. They had trouble finding it, as the snow had covered everything. Clever Daddy pressed his key ring until the lights flashed on their car. They all got in and they were just about to drive off when Anna said "Where's Cat?" Mummy gave Daddy a very worried look. "I last saw it at our feet when we hugged and kissed in the shop,' said Mummy.

"I didn't pick it up," said Daddy. Oh No. Daddy leapt out of the car and was just about to dash to the shop, when he looked down at his feet and there was Cat.

"How on earth did it get there, he said, picking it up and handing it to a thankful Anna.

"Thank you, Daddy," said Anna as she pressed it against her body.

"Oh, poor Cat you are very cold and you've got snow in your tracks. Which she brushed off with her new gloves. Daddy jumped back in the driving seat and looked at Mummy. She looked very pleased he had found it so quickly. They drove out of the car park, but had to drive very slowly, as the road was thick with snow and very slippery. "We never had this problem in Singapore" said Mummy amusingly" They slowly left the big city behind them with its bright lights. They drove along the road that was very dark. It was very difficult to see up ahead, because of all the falling snow. It began to get thicker and the wheels began to spin as they climbed a steep hill. Until they came to a halt, unable to move forward.

"What do we do now?" asked Mummy trying not to sound worried.

"If it continues to snow as much as this. We will need a digger to get us out" replied Daddy.

"I have one" said Anna picking up Cat. Daddy laughed and said he wished he had Cat's big brother. When all of a sudden, a bright light dazzled them from the road. But they couldn't see what it was as the light was shining in their faces. They heard chains being attached to the front of the car. They started moving forward but the light still shone in their faces. So, they closed their eyes and where suddenly asleep. When they woke up the light had disappeared, and there before them was their house. They all climbed out. Mummy noticed the big tracks in front of the car. But there was no sign of what had pulled them, and no tracks showing where it had gone to. Anna picked up Cat, before leaving the car. She found that it had snow on its wheels, and in its digger shovel.

"How did it get there" she thought. As she remembered cleaning it when she got into the car. Once again, she saw the headlight blink. This time the horn did a quite beep. She walked back into the house and laid Cat beside the fire. Where its arms gradually lowered and it looked as though it was asleep.

Who do you think towed the car home?

# VISITOR TWENTY-THREE -MAT THE MAGIC RED TRACTOR

Anna, had a friend called Emily who enjoyed exploring the countryside. So, one day, Emily was driven there by her mother and father to see a farm, that was at the bottom of a valley. There were high hills on either side, and a river twisting and turning, and falling from great heights into a lake below.

Before she got out of the car. She had to put on bright red wellington boots, because everywhere was thick with mud. In fact, it was so thick that her mother couldn't move the car. The farmer came out of his house. He even had problems walking, as his wellington boots, kept getting stuck in the mud.

"This is a job for the Magic Red Tractor", cried out the farmer. As he fell forward, when his feet couldn't move. All of a sudden, a roar was heard from the large garage, at the end of the farmer's house. Out came a magnificent machine with lights blazing and dazzling everyone who looked at it. It came roaring up the road and stopped in front of Emily, and rocked from side to side. To Emily's surprise she heard a rumbly sort of voice that said "Hello! Can I help you?"

Emily was not frightened but simply pointed to her mother's car. She asked if it could move it to a dry piece of land, without damaging it.

The Magic Red Tractor known as Mat, turned round on the spot. It took one look at the car, and uncoiled a rope with a hook at the end. Emily's mother, who was standing next to the car. Grabbed hold of the end and attached it to something under the engine of her car. Then Mat simply pulled the car up the road. Not once did its wheels get stuck, as they were so big with deep treads. It gave it the ability to move over the worst type of roads.

The farmer called out to Mat. "I can't reach the cows on the hills side, because of all this mud. Could you take them some cattle cake, which is a food they like very much? Then bring them down for milking."

Mat flashed the colored lights above his cab which meant Yes.

Mat then came over to Emily and towered over her. "Would you like to come with me?

"Yes please. Can mummy and daddy come to?"

"Of course, I'll go and hook up the trailer that's loaded with the cattle feed. They can sit at the back, while you sit in the cab. I will then tell you all about the farm," replied Mat.

"But mummy and daddy would like to learn all about the countryside. Can't they squeeze in the cab?"

"Aargh! I forgot to mention that I can only talk to children. Adults can't hear me, said Mat. Maybe you can tell them what you've learned. On the way back?"

"Yes, I'll do that and explain why you used your lights to say Yes to the farmer" replied Emily.

"I'll be back in jiffy." With that, he roared off to a large barn. Where he backed up, hooked up the trailer, that was very heavy. But not to Mat. By the time he came back. Emily had persuaded her parents to go for a ride to see the cows. They climbed on the back of the trailer. While Emily climbed in the cab that was full of dials, levers, and colored lights. As she sat on the seat, she found she couldn't see out. Mat told her to press the button beside her chair. As she did so, the seat began to rise, until she could see everything. Including mummy and daddy at the back of the trailer. Mat tooted his horn and off they went. Mummy and daddy nearly fell off as he went off very quickly. More like a racing car than a slow tractor. It was very comfortable for Emily, sitting on the leather seat watching the countryside speed by. But not so, for mummy and daddy, who were bouncing up and down. As the trailer went over one hole after another; poor mummy and daddy. Thought Emily who was watching them to make sure they didn't fall off.

Mat told Emily all about the trees, flowers, the birds in the hedgerows. She never realized how many different ones there were. She would never have noticed many of them if Mat hadn't pointed them out. Or stopped to let Emily creep up to a bush. To look at a mother song thrush, sitting on her eggs. Mummy and daddy were pleased every time they stopped. As they could stretch their legs and rub their bottoms that were now bruised.

They eventually arrived at the field. Where maybe, forty cows were chewing at the grass. Daddy opened the gate and Mat drove through. It went to one corner, where there were lots of containers. He backed up the trailer which then began to rise. The cow cakes began to slide into the large wooden boxes. Mat was very clever as he didn't miss one box. He then lowered the trailer and flashed all his lights and sounded his musical horn. All the cows looked up from eating, as they knew it was time to eat something special. So, they all started wandering towards the containers. Mat, Emily and her parents went out of the field and closed the gate. They then watched the cows. As you can't be too careful when around cows, as they can sometimes get upset. Especially if they have young heifers, and being so big with horns, they could easily knock you down.

Now that the rain had stopped and the sun was shining. It became a beautiful day. More so, as the view of the green countryside and the hills. With fluffy white clouds above, was an amazing sight to see. After the cattle had eaten. It was time to take them down to the milking parlor at the farm. Mat lead the way followed by the cows, that were in a long row. At the end of the row was Emily's parents, as they wanted to walk, as their bottoms couldn't stand the journey back on the trailer. What they didn't consider. Was that forty cows that had just eaten would start crapping non route. By the time they got back to the farm their boots and legs were very smelly. Emily tried not to laugh but it was a funny sight. Especially when the farmer brought out a hose and sprayed them from top to toe.

Their clothes were very wet so they borrowed some overalls from the farmer. While their clothes dried in the sunshine. They helped the farmer feed the ducks in the pond, and the chickens that ran everywhere. Emily even collected eggs from various spots around the farm. Where the hens had left them. They had an enormous lunch and afterwards. They laid on their backs on the hillside overlooking the farm and fell asleep. Emily was the first to wake up. To her surprise she saw Mat flying in the air, playing with the swallows. Mat saw she was awake and winked with one of his headlights. Then as her parents started to wake up. Mat flew to the ground and just stood still in the field opposite. Emily decided not to tell them that Mat could fly and talk. As they wouldn't have believed her. Maybe one day they would.

They put on their now dry clothes that still smelled of the countryside. They thanked the farmer for a lovely day and promised to return soon. Emily went up to Mat and gave him a big hug. She said she would persuade her parents to come back next weekend. Mat smiled and said he would show her the waterfall and the cave where there lived an escaped tiger.

Upon returning to their house. Emily went and visited Anna and Jemima and told them all about Mat. Anna, introduced her to Cat who mentally suggested that they all went with her the next time she went to the farm.

# VISITOR TWENTY-FIVE- PETERS DREAM WORLD

A man called Peter is sleeping and dreaming. He finds himself in a huge amphitheater but the lighting is so bright that he can't see if there is anyone there. He moves to the canter where there is a stage. He climbs the steps and stands in the middle shading his eyes from the brilliant lights. Suddenly, the lights go out. Except for one solitary beam that shines gently on him. He is holding a book that we see is called 'Seth Speaks'. He turns to a page and reads out loud. "Let the force within, expand to the past, present and future. For there you will meet your other selves."

He closes the book and concentrates. Slowly the lights in the amphitheater begin to appear and he sees thousands of images of individuals. But each one is in what appears to be, a bubble. He tries studying each bubble. The closer he looks in one bubble. He sees an individual that appears to be in different and multi locations. He notices that their clothes and location are of different periods in history, the present, and possibly the future. Each individual's face is the same face. Some look older, hairier, stressed, smiling, sad, angry, and so on. There is also a baby in a cot also with the same face.

Peter looks up from his book and looks amazed at what he is seeing before him. He turns full circle and the whole amphitheater is full of people who look like him. "Am I dreaming?" he calls out.

"Yes and No. Thank you for reading my books for the past twenty years. I was wondering when you would try one of the exercises." Said a voice.

"Is that Seth." Enquires Peter.

"Yes and No. I am the Seth that came to your Earthly dimension to teach you about your Reality and your sub conscious selves. I am also part of your sub conscious. Just as I was a part of Jane Roberts who I spoke through, and whose husband Robert wrote every word I said for over thirty years." Explained Seth.

"Do you have something to tell me?" asks Peter.

"Yes and No. I want you to help me to visually explain the realty you experience and how. By listening to your sub conscious, that some on Earth call their soul. You can change the world you are experiencing now." Replied Seth

"Hold on. You want little old me to change the world."

"Yes and No. Everyone creates their own world but they don't know it. Nor do they realize that before coming to this time and place on Earth. They agreed with millions of other souls to join them and to see and experience what they are experiencing. But each soul actually sees things ever so slightly differently."

"So, millions of other souls on this Earth have planned to change this world we now live in?"

"Yes and No. There are millions who are unhappy with the direction this world is headed. But they feel helpless in doing anything about it. You and everyone else has the ability to communicate with them all at soul level, and agree how to change the world."

"How on earth do I contact millions of other souls, if I don't have their email or phone number?

"You meet them all the time in your dream state."

"Blimey, no wonder I feel knackered when I wake up in the morning."

"Very funny, but not all that wrong, as you have been astral travelling for many years now. Last night you spent time in Russia and Japan before returning to Sosua. Plus, meeting with hundreds of friends in other countries.

"That can't be right. I went to bed around midnight. Then went to the loo at least three times. No way could I have travelled that far."

"How many times have you read in my books. That time does not exist in the dream world. What you think, happens instantly, including meeting old friends in England."

"If time doesn't exist. How old am I, when I meet my friends?"

"Whatever age you want to be, and likewise your friend can see you the age they want you to be."

"Hang on a minute. If there is no time in dreamland can I meet someone I met, in another lifetime? I read in your books that we experience the physical earth many times?"

"You do indeed and as time does not exist 'Everything' is instantaneous, which I admit is difficult to get your head around. Especially, the concept that you can meet your friends in the future also.

"Can you prove it?"

PETER'S OTHER SELVES

"Let me start by introducing you to your other selves. I'll begin with a version of you when you were 18 years old in this lifetime."

Seth showed Peter a young man in a suit, running as fast as he can from his office passed a dock in Hull, into the town centre. He keeps looking at his watch, until he stops at a corner of a street. From where he hides looking across the street to where various office workers are exiting. Suddenly, a girl appears and he goes weak at the knees. He sees her coming towards the corner, so he runs like mad back down the street to the next corner and keeps running. Then stops, combs his hair and casually walks back towards the street. Where to his surprise he meets the girl, as she rounds the corner. The girl is his first love and he can't miss a day without seeing her when he was a young man.

"Wow what a surprise meeting you here. I have something to tell you. Can you spare a minute?" asks the 18-year-old Peter.

"Yes, I have an hour, let me pick up a sandwich first and we can go sit in the gardens." They buy some sandwiches then walk to a near bye park, by a pond, where they sit.

"I've been offered a job in our Felixstowe office. Which is about a hundred and fifty miles away." Says Peter.

"That means I won't see you each day." Explains the girl.

"That's why I wanted to see you now. You have a boyfriend who you care for and may marry one day. I am just a friend who cares for you so much that I am in agony, if I don't see you each day. You don't know this. But every evening I drive on my scooter the three miles to your house and pass by two or three times in the hope I catch a glimpse of you.

"Oh! Peter you are such a nice person and fun to be with. I'm so sorry your leaving as I will miss you."

"Augh! It is such an opportunity to further my career, that I must take it. I leave tomorrow.

"Oh! so soon. May I come to the station to see you off

"I would love that. You can then meet my parents." The following day Peter introduces her to his parents. He then hugs them all and kisses her for the first time, on the lips, who hands him a letter. Everyone is crying.

"I've known and loved you for a year. But that is the first time I've kissed you. I will never forget you or stop loving you." Declares 18-year-old Peter.

"Please read the letter as I feel the same and will always remember you." Replies the girl who does marry her boyfriend and has three daughters.

"You know when you told her that you had another job. What where your thoughts at that moment." Asks Seth.

"I so wanted her to say. Not to go. Had she done so; I would have asked her to marry me." Said Peter.

"In my books. I've told you that every thought happens. If the emotion is strong enough you create a version of yourself that goes and experiences the thought. Let me show you." Explains Seth.

Peter enters a different bubble where the girl is sitting on the same seat in the park and asks him not to go. He proposes to her and they get married and buy a house in Hull. She gives birth to two boys. Peter becomes a shipping manager and they all travel together around the world.

Seth tells him "I can show you thousands of lives that you have lived on this visit to Earth. Plus, visits in the past, future, and other dimensions including the one you mistakenly call death. Look around you as these are all your other selves,"

Peter goes and peeps into some of the bubbles and at one-point jumps back in surprise. Saying to Seth "

Wait a minute there's a woman in there that looks like me."

"Of course, you come back in all forms to experience as many aspects of Earthly life as you can. That's before you decide not to return again as a human. You then may experience a different dimension. It's up to you."

"Are you telling me that I've come back as a woman?" Seth suggests he studies the many other bubbles. Where Peter sees he appears as a: - lesbian, a monk, a slave, a king, a fighter pilot, a bank robber being chased, a policeman being shot while chasing a bank robber, a spaceman in the future landing on Venus. Plus, many other situations.

PETER'S SHOWN ANOTHER DIMENSION

"Would you like to see your soul in another dimension." Asks Seth.

"I suppose so." He replies but he is apprehensive, as he is overwhelmed at what he has been seeing. He is suddenly taken back to the creation of Earth as an amoeba experiencing water. He then becomes a Tyrannous Rex roaring, as he fights another prehistoric animal. He then becomes an eagle happily gliding on an air current before laying on a tree branch.

"That was your soul experiencing other life forms that are of a different frequency/dimension to that of humans. That is why prehistoric man, and aborigines respected and communicated with nature as they contained what they called spirits. I assume you realize that you also experienced being the tree that the Eagle landed on?" suggests Seth.

Peter replies saying that 'Somehow, I sensed that. Maybe that's why I hug and talk to trees and plants and try not to harm a living thing.

"It's also why you wrote the children's stories.' The Secret World of the Plant People'" explains Seth.

"Are the different dimensions always on this planet?" enquires Peter.

"Far from it. There are millions of dimensions you can choose to experience."

"Is Earth a popular choice?

"Far from it, very few energies/souls choose to experience the confines of Earth."

"What do you mean by confines?"

"Earth is unique, as I suppose, all other dimensions are. But you are far more restricted in what you can do and achieve."

"If I had lots of money. I could do anything."

"You don't need money to change the world."

"What do I need then?"

"The ability to knowingly manipulate energy to create and change your world."

"Show me what you mean." Instructs Peter.

PETER'S DREAM

He is lying in bed having this mental conversation with Seth. The room has a window to his left, a door to the right in the corner. There is a fitted wardrobe at the bottom of the bed. A guitar is on a stand to the left of the wardrobe. A picture of the Beatles hangs on one wall, and on another a super model.

"Hang on to the bed as this is going to be some journey." Instructs Seth.

"Don't forget I'm not wearing any pants." Claims Peter.

"Are you sure about that?' asks Seth. Peter looks under the sheets and sees he is fully clothed. He is suddenly amazed as everything in the room changes position. The window with curtains shut, moves to the right of the room, and the curtains open to bright sun light. The door moves onto the ceiling and its open slightly. He can see the moon as though it was next door. Paul from the Beatles steps out of the picture and picks up Peter's guitar and asks if he can borrow it, as his string has just broken. Paul looks at the super model and says "I hope you have as much fun with her as I did" He then walks back into the picture where the other three are cracking jokes. As he returns, Ringo starts to play the drums and soon all four are playing "She Loves You" with Paul using Peter's guitar.

Then the super model steps out of the picture and says. "Paul told me to show you a good time, Big boy. Which club shall we go to first? I know" she says and grabs Peter's hand who is now dressed like a 60s mod. She opens the wardrobe door and they go through into a very lively night club where the Rolling Stones are playing. All around are faces he recognizes from his teenage days in the 60s. They all call out as he passes each one. "Hi Peter. Pleased you could make it". The music changes to a slow seductive rhythm and he finds himself dancing cheek to cheek with the super model. Suddenly, Peter finds himself back in his bed and the room is back to how it was. He starts crying and asks Seth to be taken back immediately.

"You can go back at any time. All you need to do is to learn how to manipulate energy. Which is what we do all the time." Explains Seth.

"Who is we, and sign me up for the course." Instructs Peter.

'We' is every energy that has ever existed in the past, present and the future. Including, you."

"What do you mean 'me'. I tell you if I could manipulate energy. I would be with that model day and night.

"Before you chose to be 'Peter' in this lifetime. You did what I just did and actually created the world you have been experiencing since being borne.

"Do you mean I chose to be borne in Hull, fail my exams, be a workaholic, two divorces, and penniless in the Caribbean?" asked Peter.

"Plus, making friends, falling in love, succeeding in the job you liked, travelling to many countries, and studying the esoteric when you were 40 years old.' Explains Seth.

"Okay, I accept that I've had some wonderful moments, including writing, but there were times I was not happy."

"That's why you've you chosen to revisit the Earth dimension many times. You wanted to experience all forms of emotions."

"Surely, I didn't choose physical pain?"

"Of course, you did. As an Energy all sensations are valid and to be experienced. In this and many other worlds. We don't experience emotions as you do on Earth.

"I must be bonkers wanting to keep returning to Earth."

"Not bonkers but all visitors are considered heroes as the emotions they feel add to the knowledge of the universes."

"You're telling me that if I break my toe, the world experiences my pain?

"No. But the experience and the way you handle it is unique. It will never be repeated identically by anyone else. Let me show you."

SOLDIERS AT WAR.

A group of soldiers are in the trenches waiting to go over the top at the break of dawn. Some are writing to their loved ones at home, each letter being very personal to the writer and recipient. One officer is writing to his teenage son, telling him not to enlist. Another, reminding his sweetheart of the times spent together. Another, writing to his mother and apologizing for leaving her alone and joining the army. Others are just talking. As they need the company, as they are afraid of what might happen to them at dawn.

Come the morning, they fix bayonets and wait the command to advance. It comes and these brave soldiers climb to the top of the trenches. Where almost all of them are cut down and killed by the enemies' machine guns. The soldier who wrote to his sweetheart dodges the bullets and even helps to carry back some injured to the trench, when ordered to return. One of the injured is the one who wrote apologizing to his mother. He is badly wounded and returned to England where he is nursed by his mother in the hospital. The soldier who rescued him is promoted and given a bravery medal, which he one day sends to sweetheart. With the message "thinking of you always, and waiting for the moment when we are together again." He survives the war, gets married and the injured soldier is his best man.

The officer is killed but saves the life of his son, who hesitates to join up, and the war ends just before he feels he must do so for King and country.

"It may interest you to know that the officer elected to return to Earth immediately." Says Seth.

"Did he know he had been violently killed?" asks Peter.

"Yes, which is why he returned so that come the next war. He tried to persuade people not to fight. He was arrested and chose to help the injured soldiers instead of prison'. After the war he became a politician to try and stop future wars happening.

"I'm surprised more didn't come back over" comments Peter.

"Oh! but they did. Millions in fact who met up before coming over to see how they could prevent wars.

"They didn't do a very good job." Suggested Peter.

"They are still trying, and continue to return until the human race realizes that everything is connected and they reach a new level of awareness.

"Are you one of them?

No. replies Seth. I'm here to educate and to remind those that did go over, and why they chose this journey. That's why I'm talking to you now.

"What? Me change the world you must be crazy. I'm 70, live on an island, no money, and don't know anyone of influence.

"Just like most of the others. I'll introduce you to them."

"Not here surely, I've only got a studio apartment."

"Yes, here in your small apartment, I'll bring over a million to talk to you tomorrow night."

"What, wait, I only have one packet of biscuits and five tea bags."

You don't realize that you will all meet in another dimension in your room. It will actually look like an auditorium. Where dreamers appear next to other dreamers from where they live in the physical human world. I will suggest they give those sitting close to them their human contact details. So, that when they stop dreaming and return to the physical world. They can meet with each other, say at coffee bars, and work together to change the physical world. At least one member will have psychic/medium abilities and remind the others about their meeting in the dreamworld. That they will revisit on a number of occasions to meet with others around the world. Wanting to prevent wars, connecting with mother nature where they will help and protect all living things, and change the environment to one where everyone enjoys living.

Also, like the Lumerians, who existed in the human world before the stone age. They will develop methods of creating food, so they don't have to kill animals. You may realize that dreamed children entering Plant world with their skills and talents. Are actually entering a semi physical world where they care and communicate with all animals.

This is different from the world they will enter when they physically die, and leave the physical human world. If you read Section Two of my book 'Seth Speaks' written by Jane Roberts and published by Amber-Allen. You will learn all about the 'Death' Experience and 'Death' conditions in life.

I recently re-read the whole book as I'm over seventy and experiencing a number of painful physical problems. I realize it's an experience I am learning about, but I was wondering if I will be moving to another dimension. So, I reread Section Two of Seth Speaks so that I will move to the dimension with positive knowledgeable thoughts. So that I can immediately enjoy the amazing happy dimension and meet up with all my family and friends who already moved there. I can also create any images of a world I want to enjoy living in.

After reading the Seth books you will also find ways of changing your physical world and how to visit other dimensions in your dreams.

# APPENDIX -

Uncle Twotrees. The Plant World leader who often visits different dimensions, such as, the human world. He took me to 'The World of Imagination.' where he introduced me to some plastic ducks, and my Dominican Penguins that began talking to me. (You can read about the visit in my book 'The Secret World of Dream Children' Chapter 44. You will also be able to read about my Dominican Penguins, Dominican Cats and Dogs in my next series of photo books where the animals describe what is happening in each photo.)

Uncle Twotrees took me to another dimension and introduced me to an amazing character called Seth. He is ai educator that visits many dimensions whose purpose is to help guide everyone in their world. In the 1960s- 1980s he often visited the human world where he explained about everything in the human world. He did this by working with Jane Roberts, the medium, who he mentally took over. Her husband recorded everything he said and published over nine amazing books that I have read and continually study. I suggest you start by reading 'Seth Speaks' by Jane Roberts, published by Amber-Allen Publishing. I suggest you also study the following site:

I About Sethcenter.com, New Awareness Network Inc. and The Seth Educational Institute

Started in 1988 by Rick Stack, New Awareness Network Inc. is the publisher of approximately 2/3 of the existing Seth books by Jane Roberts and is the exclusive publisher of the Seth Audio Collection, actual recordings of Seth recorded by Rick in Jane Roberts' Classes in the 1970's.The Seth Educational Institute provides learning and enrichment activities for both long time Seth readers and new readers alike. These activities, including ongoing online Seth classes, online Seth courses, Seth Conferences, live classes and educational materials, will be designed to help people use their own resources to actualize their dreams, explore inner reality, and awaken to a greater understanding of themselves and the multi-dimensional universe. Further, the Seth Educational Institute will endeavor to introduce people throughout the globe to the wisdom and practical applications contained within the Seth material.

Contact our office: sumari@sethcenter.com

Customer Service New Awareness Network Inc. The Seth Bookstore and Audio Collection. The Seth Educational Institute. https://sethcenter.com/

Email: sumari@sethcenter.com

# Don't miss out!

Visit the website below and you can sign up to receive emails whenever Peter Brighton publishes a new book. There's no charge and no obligation.

https://books2read.com/r/B-A-PWSK-XSGCC

**BOOKS 2 READ**

Connecting independent readers to independent writers.

Did you love *Young Adults Visit Other Dimensions*? Then you should read *Three Strangers Rob a Gangster*[1] by Peter Brighton!

There are two spiritual guides called Micael and Casiel, in the 5th dimension. Trying to bring together the following strangers. In order to help a priest, called Father Eamon. To prevent a London gangster called Vince McCreedy from demolishing the churches day center.

Jenny- A former tax inspector and now working for a major investment bank. She has a handicapped son called Gary.

Chris Hawkins- a good looking computer systems analyst. He is an expert at preventing hackers entering his client's computers.

Tom Darwin- an accountant unwillingly working for the violent gangster Vince McCreedy.

Read more at https://petersbooklets.com/.

---

1. https://books2read.com/u/3LwVX1

2. https://books2read.com/u/3LwVX1

# About the Author

My writers name is Peter Brighton. I'm a 73-year-old retired Brit, living alone in the Dominican Republic. I spend most of my time writing children's stories, film and TV scripts. Plus, a series of self-printing photo booklets of an owner's pets. I add comments, by the pet, under each photo, sent to me by the owner. I also have a series of photo booklets about 'Dominican penguins, cats, dogs and other animals'.

Please visit my website www.petersbooklets.com for more information. Especially, if you read one of my stories, that you believe is like you or your child. I can then try and send you a personalized self-printing booklet, with your picture on the cover. You can then print as many copies as you want and send to friends. Or simply forward by email or WhatsApp.

My objective in life. Is to help people move their lives forward. Also, to help stray dogs and cats. If I become a successful writer. I shall use the royalties, to help more people and animals.

I am also trying to encourage young adults to read, Seth, the spiritual guide and teacher, books by Jane Roberts. If you read 'page 328 of the book 'Seth Speaks' you will learn that Christ will be returning in 2075 to change the worlds religions. By studying the Seth books, you will be able to help him.

Read more at https://petersbooklets.com/,.